Sharon

Vladimir's Victory

Leigh M. Hall

D1527698

Vladimir's Victory

A spin-off story of the full novel,

This Family Sucks! Sincerely Yours, Peter Frazier.

ASIN: B09PGPZR9B
LMH Publications 2022

Contents

Vladimir's Victory

A Frazier Family

Short Story

Written By: Leigh M. Hall

This is a short story, spin-off from the full-length novel, This Family Sucks! Sincerely Yours, Peter Frazier

If you have not read the full novel, I highly recommend reading it before continuing with this story.

This Family Sucks! Sincerely Yours, Peter Frazier can be found on Amazon and Audible.

Chapter One

Mary Beth and Michael Frazier have seven children; Vladimir falls somewhere in the middle. Being in the middle of this several-layer sandwich, you have to be extra spicy in order to stand out. Vladimir is what one would call eccentric; living in a small Texas town, the slightest difference could make you an exile., but since Vladimir is a Frazier, he is respected despite his differences.

At the age of twenty-two, he has settled into a routine. Just last year, he was made manager of Pet Palace, the place he has worked at since high school. Not an accomplishment most people strive for, but Vladimir is happy with his life so far. Once he got the promotion and was handed the reins of the Tyler branch, he got his very first apartment. Just a small one-bedroom within the city limits and close to work, but it was home to him. His parents helped him furnish the place; it wasn't much trouble since most of the space was filled with his atriums and tanks. Vladimir's reptile collection has grown immensely, so much so that he has to remind himself that he is currently out of room and bringing home any more pets is out of the question.

With his new position, his new place, and the responsibility he has to all his snakes, Vladimir rarely has time for a social life these days. Sure, he still gets out from time to time. Even though he is now the manager, he is still close with his coworkers. He tries really hard at not becoming an ass like his predecessor; the staff at Pet Palace couldn't stand that guy. His best friend, Stewart, used to work with him but had recently moved on and gotten a job at his father's construction company. However, he still makes time to join the old gang on Friday nights for drinks at The Railroad. The crew would stick around till they couldn't stand, then head off in their separate sections of the world for the remainder of the night.

Vladimir had been so busy with all the changes in his life that he hadn't had a chance to date anyone since... well, he couldn't remember when. He was young, but that wouldn't last forever. He did want to find someone to share his life with at some point, but he also wanted to have some fun while he did it. The thing is, he was getting tired of it always being about the fun. He had never had a steady girlfriend, and he longed for that connection; the same connection he saw from some of his friends, his sisters, and his parents. Perhaps it was ingrained in him after being the product of his parents' love and seeing the way they interacted over the years.

He hadn't thought about it much until now, but he was sure that was just what he wanted in life. The problem was, living in a small town didn't give him many options.

The debacle that his family went through a couple of years ago gave him a new perspective on life. Also, seeing his siblings, Tallulah and Peter, almost hook up made him realize that he needed to find someone fast before every eligible female was taken. He didn't want to be left in the predicament that they had been in; the thought made him internally cringe. Good thing that phase was over. Tallulah had gone off to OSU to start college, and Peter was happy with his day-to-day routine at Frazier Firearms.

Vladimir had offered to have either Elan or Peter move in with him. They could be roommates and share the cost of living. He didn't need it, the rent was cheap, and his pay was more than enough to cover it. He just wanted someone else there and thought they might want to get out of the house. Neither one of them took him up on the offer. Michael had said they couldn't stay forever, and eventually he was going to start charging them rent. Elan is now twenty-eight, and if they haven't started charging him yet, he doubted they will start any time soon.

His parents couldn't hold out forever; this was Michael's last year as a working man, as he plans to retire after Christmas. Sure, he will still oversee the shop—it is his shop—but as far as going in every day, that's not going to happen anymore. He and Mary Beth are ready for the retired life. They have raised seven children, and it is time to move on to the next phase in life. Mary Beth had a tough time recovering from the Trent incident, they all did, but she took it the hardest. A lot of therapy was had after the summer of 1996, but she is getting by okay now, at least that's what Vladimir thinks.

Elan took it almost as hard as his mother; he didn't date for over a year, and that's saying a lot for Elan. He was never one to be without a pretty little thing under his arm. Seeing him sulk around with his tail between his legs was hard. Eventually, he got past it. He just got up one morning and decided he wasn't going to let the loss of Trish and his unborn child affect him anymore. There was nothing he could do about the past but everything he can do about the future.

Vladimir is working the evening shift with Evette Ramos today. She is new, only started about a month ago, but at eighteen she is a good worker. She does well with the animals and has even shown some interest in grooming, which is always helpful around the pet store. They only have one groomer, Nelia Patel, but she works full time at another job and can't come in every day. So every chance Evette gets, she is working with Nelia, trying to learn the ins and outs so she can maybe take over full-time someday.

It is time to start closing up when a young couple enter the store. "Ugh," Evette complains from behind the register while glancing at the clock on the wall.

"Sorry, five more minutes. We must give them a chance to shop. If they haven't made a purchase at ten after, you can make the closing announcement," Vladimir says.

"That means I can't close my till until after they leave," she whines.

"Relax, it's not like we stay open late. Eight is still early; you could go work at Brookshire and get off at eleven," Vladimir reminds her in a teasing tone.

"No, thank you! I am good right here; my mother would never let me stay out that late. I may be eighteen, but I am still in school and still have to follow her rules," Evette rolls her eyes at the end of her statement. "Go start doing your closing thing, so those people know they need to hurry."

"You got it, boss," Vladimir says with laughter but gets to work pulling in the displays that sit outside the door.

The couple that came in are not familiar with either of the two working. They peruse the aisles as if they are looking for nothing in particular.

After a few minutes, Evette and Vladimir can hear hushed arguing coming from the back, over by the bulk dog food. Evette gives Vladimir a worried look, but he just holds up a finger indicating to give them a minute. It is now five past eight, and Evette is losing her patience.

"Just fucking pick one already! It's a dog, for fuck's sake, he will literally eat garbage," the man's voice echoes throughout the empty store.

"Don't yell at me. I just want what's best for him. I need to read the ingredients to make sure he isn't getting anything toxic," the girl's hushed reply is much quieter but still bounces off the walls.

Evette gives Vladimir a startled look, so he decides to do something. "I will go see if they need some help. You stay here," Vladimir instructs.

"You guys need some assistance?" Vladimir asks as he approaches the couple.

"No, just getting some dog food. Why are there so many options? It's just dog food, for God's sake," the irritated man complains.

"Well, different food for different dogs and different stages. What do you guys have?" Vladimir asks in a polite tone. At six foot three with dyed black hair and pale skin, he is a sight, one that can be intimidating. The asshole that was hollering at his girlfriend does not seem bothered even though he stands at least four inches shorter than Vladimir.

"We have a dog," the man answers, shrugging his shoulders with indifference.

"No, Jalal, it is not a dog. He is a puppy." She looks over at Vladimir with an apologetic expression and says, "He is a puppy. We found him this morning in our apartment complex. No one claimed him, so I guess we are stuck with him for a little bit. I am not sure what breed, but he is small, like really small. He has teeth, though, so I think we can give him the dry stuff. I am going to make up some flyers when I can get to Kinkos tomorrow, but until we find his owners, I don't want him to go hungry."

"I told her we aren't keeping him. He can stay out on the balcony as long as he stays quiet, but that's it. I don't even think we can have a dog in our apartment," Jalal states.

"What apartment complex do you live in?" Vladimir enquires.

"What's it to you? You gonna come take him for a walk or something?" Jalal's snide remark makes the girl grimace.

"Don't be so rude," she says.

"Can it, Carrisa, I'll be whatever I want to be. You got me up in here spending my hard-earned money on a mutt, so don't go catching attitude with me in front of a stranger."

Vladimir clears his throat, "I only ask because I am familiar with the pet policies in almost all the complexes around here, so I might be able to let you know if you can keep him or not."

Jalal stops him by holding up a hand, "No need, we aren't keeping him. If she doesn't find a home for him soon, he has got to go, and I don't care where that is."

"Okay, well, he is a puppy, and I see that you are not picky, and he is most likely a stray, so some Puppy Chow might suffice for now. I recommend you get a couple cans of wet food and mix it in with the dry food, it will help with the digestion." Vladimir pulls a five-pound bag off the shelf; one he hopes is in their price range, then two cans off another. "Will this work?"

Jalal eyes the items and the price, then says, "Yeah, I can manage that."

Carrisa jumps up and down with glee, "Oh, thank you, love." She then wraps her arms around Jalal and gives him a long kiss on the cheek.

Vladimir hadn't paid much attention to her before that moment. She is short, maybe five-four, but she is wearing knee-high Docs that give her an extra inch. When she kissed her boyfriend, she had to stretch up onto her toes and reach her neck out as far as it would go. Jalal didn't move in to help her any. As Vladimir eyes her, he can feel Jalal watching him. When he looks back, Jalal has a deadly expression on his face. Vladimir turns and starts walking toward the register with the dog food still in his hands.

"You guys were just in time; we were about to close up. Come on, and I will ring you for the items. Do you have a rewards card?"

"What's that?" Carrisa asks.

"It is something new. You get a discount on all purchases made in the store. It's really easy." Vladimir pulls out the little paper that customers need to fill out in order to get the rewards card and sits it on the counter.

Carrisa leans in to start filling it out, but Jalal stops her. "We don't need that; we are not keeping the dog."

"Still, it will save you ten percent on your purchase today," Vladimir says as he gives Evette a look saying he has this and starts ringing up the items.

"Why do we need a card to save? Why can't the price just be ten percent lower?" Jalal asks.

Vladimir shrugs, "Got me, just policy, I don't own the store, I just work here."

By the time Vladimir has rung up the three items, Carrisa has filled out the card and hands it over. "Doesn't hurt anything to have the card," she says.

"Only now they have your info," Jalal retorts.

"Oh, so they can come rob us for our twenty-inch television and decade-old stereo?" She teases, but Jalal does not look happy.

Vladimir pipes in before a fight can break out, "Okay, here is your card," he says, handing it over, "Your total is nine dollars and sixteen cents.

Jalal hands over a ten-dollar bill and waits for his change. Carrisa picks up the bag while looking excited.

"Y'all enjoy that puppy while you have him. I am sure he needs lots of love after being left out on his own." The steam coming off of Jalal from Vladimir's words is almost visible.

"Oh, I plan on it. You should smell his breath. It is the most amazing smell ever!" Carrisa jumps up and down as she exits the store, her boots echoing in her wake.

Vladimir stands there and stares at the door for several minutes after they have exited the store. The spiky pixie hair that's dyed platinum blond with black roots are now ingrained in his brain. Her small figure would fit perfectly in his hands. He could bend and flip her all over the damn place as she giggles and bounces just as she had done moments ago. He could give her joy, that same joy that was written all over her face when she talked about the puppy.

"Hello, Earth to Vlad. Are you in there?" Evette asks while waving her hands around in front of him.

"Sorry, I spaced out there for a minute. What's up?"

Evette lets out a knowing laugh, "What's up? I want to go home. That's what's up. Can we close the damn store now?"

"Of course, what are you waiting on?"

"Right, okay. Whatever you say, Casanova." Evette closes out her till while Vladimir eyes the rewards card Carrisa filled out.

Carrisa Abbott, that is a pretty name, Vladimir thinks, *it suits her*. Also written on the card is her address and phone number. It would be against policy for him to use it. He knows this. But what if he just wanted to check on the puppy, see if they found its owner yet. That wouldn't be so bad, would it?

Chapter Two

Sunday night has arrived. The store closes at six on Sundays, so Vladimir always has plenty of time to make it to the weekly family dinner. The crowd had dwindled down a bit over the years. After Bethany's death, no one was in the mood for a gathering, but Mary Beth was adamant at keeping to tradition.

Nigel, Thomas, Elan, Vladimir, Michael, Mary Beth, and Peter are always present. Poppy rarely comes up from Houston anymore. She is busy with adult life in the city. Phoebe and Mark don't make it every week, with Hannah having just turned four. She keeps them busy with extracurriculars, and their newborn Stephan is a bit of a handful. Mary Beth gets to see them plenty during the week, maybe more than she wants to see them considering Phoebe is always asking for help. Penn is off playing pro-ball; he had been traded to the Green Bay Packers this last season and rarely makes it home. It is always fun to see him when he comes close by for an away game.

Then there is Tallulah. It took her some time to recoup after the whole Trent fiasco, but she has settled into her sophomore year nicely up at Oklahoma State. Everyone in the family still dotes over her hand and foot. Whenever Tallulah needs something, it is handed over times ten. She and Peter are still best friends, despite the intimacy that had almost happened between them. He visits her whenever he can. Things were awkward for all of a second, but that didn't last long. They were back in the swing of things as if nothing had happened in no time.

Tonight, it is just the regulars at the dinner table. Mary Beth had made meatloaf, enough to feed an army because, well, she is basically feeding an army. Vladimir walks in just in time to smack Peter in the head before he can move out of his reach. It was weird at first, when they all found out about the switched at birth thing and how Peter wasn't their actual sibling, but they got past it just as they do everything else.

"You smell like shit!" Peter exclaims.

"Well, I did just clean out a dozen hamster and guinea pig cages, so I assume you are correct," Vladimir smiles at his little brother.

"Vlad, get in here and wash up before you cause your brother to break out in hives!" Mary Beth hollers from the kitchen.

"Coming, Mother!"

Elan is setting the table as Vladimir passes him, and they give each other a fist bump. Ever since Vladimir had moved out, they don't see much of each other except on Sunday nights at The Railroad. But that stopped a couple of months ago for some reason. Vladimir hadn't had a chance to ask him what the reason was, but now was the perfect opportunity.

Once Vladimir returns to the dining room after washing up, he asks Elan about it. "So, I haven't seen you at the road lately. What have you been up to, big bro?"

"I've been busy," comes Elan's short reply.

"Vague much?" Vladimir says.

Peter enters the room and adds, "Come on, Elan, cough it up. Who's the girl?" They can all hear Michael's recliner closing at Peter's words. Michael doesn't have much interest in anything, but he is all ears when it comes to his kids and who they are dating, especially after the Trent and Tallulah thing.

"It's nothing, just drop it," Elan spouts.

Michael enters the room. "What girl?"

"Elan has a girlfriend, Elan has a girlfriend," Vladimir singsongs, in an attempt to tease his brother.

"Give it a rest, will you? They just started dating; she isn't technically his girlfriend yet," Mary Beth pipes in as she sets a platter down on the table. "You guys get the rest of the food out; your grandfathers will be here any second."

"You have a girl, Elan? Why does your mother know about this, and I don't?" Michael asks his oldest son.

"Because she knows everything, Dad. Hell, she probably set the whole thing up," Peter says.

"I did no such thing. Addy is a wonderful girl, and I don't need y'all teasing him about this. I am wondering when she is going to grace us with her presence and come to a family dinner though," Mary Beth stares at Elan for a moment but he won't meet her gaze.

"Wait, Addy? Where do I know that name from? Do I know her?" Vladimir directs this question to Peter since he seems to have some answers.

"Yeah, I think you guys were the same year in high school. She used to work over at Brookshire with Elan. I'm surprised they never hooked up then." Everyone is quiet after Peter speaks. They know why it never happened with Addy and Elan back then. Because back then, Elan was with Trish. Trish, who was pregnant. Trish, who has been dead for over two years now.

Just then, Thomas and Nigel enter the house and break up the tension that had started to build. The family eats their dinner with the usual banter. No one mentions Elan's alleged girlfriend again. No karaoke is had tonight; they haven't done that in a while. It just seems silly now that Bethany isn't around to heckle everyone.

With dinner done and everyone off to their evening activities, Vladimir sneaks off to his old bedroom. It is now somewhat of a gym, if you could call a treadmill and a set of hand weights a gym. It has a phone, and that is all Vladimir needs. His parents' house has the ability to star sixty-seven someone. Meaning he can call out, and the name on the caller ID will come up as unavailable, versus 'Michael Frazier'. He doesn't have that option at his apartment.

Vladimir pulls out the information card he has been carrying around for the last couple of days, the one that has Carrisa Abbott's information on it. Yes, that's right, he kept the card. He knew it was wrong, knew he could get in trouble for it, but he didn't care. That spunky little chick has stuck with him—he can't get her out of his mind. Vladimir is nervous about making the call, has been contemplating it all weekend. He figures it is worth a try to reach out. If that asshole boyfriend of hers answers, he will just hang up. If he pulls a star sixty-nine, he can pick up before anyone else in the house and then hang up on his ass.

It's go time, now or never. The couple said they wouldn't be keeping the puppy, so calling a week later would be suspicious. He picks up the phone and dials without giving it another thought.

Carrisa answers on the second ring, "Hello," comes her cheerful greeting.

"Hi, um, is Carrisa there?" Vladimir knows it's her but still feels the need to ask.

"This is she!" Carrisa announces.

"Hello, Carrisa. My name is Vladimir. I work at the Pet Palace in Tyler. You came in two days ago and filled out a rewards membership. You had a puppy, and I just wanted to check in and see how he is doing and if you ever found the owners."

"Oh, hi! Are you the guy that helped us pick out food the other night?" Carrisa asks.

"That would be me," Vladimir replies.

"I didn't know y'all check-in; that's so cool. Yeah, um, I mean no, we never found the owners. I can only assume that the poor boy was dumped by some asshole human. He is so sweet; you should see him. I still don't know what he is, but he is really good."

"Have you named him?" Vladimir asks. He can hear her shuffling around, and then a tiny bark comes in through the line. "Is that him?"

"Yeah, we're playing right now. My boyfriend isn't home, so I'm on the living room floor with him. Jalal doesn't like him being inside. I don't blame him. The little pup has already pooped and peed on the carpet several times. I haven't named him because I can't keep him, but I've been calling him Tooter."

"Tooter? What kind of name is that?"

"Well, I know this sounds gross, but he farts, like a lot. And it's loud, and it stinks really bad," Carrisa explains.

"That might have something to do with his diet. How is he doing with the Puppy Chow?"

"Okay, I guess. I haven't had a puppy in a really long time. Well, actually, like ever. My mom had a dog when I was younger, but I was never responsible for taking care of him, so I don't know much. He has gone through all the wet food. He eats like a lot. More than I thought he would for being so little. I've been adding water to the dry food trying to soften it up for him. Jalal said he isn't buying any more food for him. He said the little dude has to go by the end of the week. So, I am trying to stretch out the food we already have."

"Can you come by the store tomorrow? You can bring the puppy with you. Let me take a look at him. Nelia is a vet tech, and she will be in from two till five tomorrow afternoon. She works full-time at the animal hospital, so she only comes in a couple of times a week. She could look him over and make sure he doesn't have any digestion issues. Everyone farts, even dogs, but it shouldn't be excessive." Vladimir cannot believe he is talking about dog farts with the most interesting girl he has met in years.

"Oh, I don't know. Jalal works till six, and he has the car all day. I could probably walk; it's not that far. The only thing is I can't afford a vet," Carrisa admits.

"First of all, she is not a vet she is a vet tech, but at Pet Palace, she is just a groomer. We wouldn't charge you. We just want to make sure he is eating the right food. Some dogs have sensitive stomachs, and they make special food for that. If you do decide to walk, make sure you let Tooter walk with you. A little exercise will do him good." He didn't need to ask her how far away she was from the store; he had her address and already knew it was less than two miles. If it was any more than that, he would offer to give her a ride.

"Okay, that sounds good! I do need to get him out some more to ask if anyone knows him. We will see you tomorrow. Thank you for checking in, Vladimir."

"My pleasure, goodnight, Carrisa."

When he hangs up, he immediately smacks himself in the head. *What the hell are you thinking*? Vladimir thinks to himself. *This chick has a boyfriend, a not-so-nice one at that.* Oh, well, too late now.

Chapter Three

Before his shift the next day, Vladimir takes extra care in his appearance. Hair perfectly slicked back, cologne on, just enough, not too much. Guyliner in place (yes, this man wears guyliner). He is a little chipper clocking in, and everyone around him notices. Arleen is working the register; Evette will relieve her at three once she gets out of school. As soon as he walks through the door, Arleen lets out a whistle.

"Well, look at you, Mister Big Shot. Somebody must have gotten some action last night. It's about damn time!" Arleen calls out. Vladimir stops and takes a look around. "Relax, there aren't any customers in here right now, just me and old Philip. He's in the back right now. So, what's got you all peppy? Did I get it right?"

"Unfortunately, no, you did not; I just happen to be in a good mood. Is that a crime?"

"For your doom-filled ass, yes. Marilyn Manson himself could have walked in here wearing a tutu and jumping rope, and it still wouldn't have been as surprising as what I just witnessed." Arleen is an older lady who works the day shift; she is a hoot, at least to herself.

"Whatever, get back to work," Vladimir slumps his shoulders then heads for the back of the store to greet Philip.

"And there's that doom. Oh, come on, don't lose your good mood on my account. I was just teasing." Vladimir waves her off and keeps walking.

He keeps busy by checking inventory and stocking shelves. Every time the door chimes, indicating that a customer is entering, he pops his head out and takes a look. As soon as Nelia arrives at two o'clock, he fills her in on the abandoned pup. She had spent that morning at the veterinary hospital and is tired, but she is also excited to play with a puppy. She had to assist in putting down a dog earlier, and the puppy will help her think of happier things.

Checking out animals is not something they do at Pet Palace; it also isn't something Vladimir had ever offered before, but there is something about Carrisa that makes him want to help her. She looks punk rock but also gives off this carefree fairy vibe. He didn't like the way her boyfriend had acted that day and felt like he needed to reach out in any way that he could.

At three-fifteen, the door chimes for the hundredth time that day, and Vladimir drags his ass out to the center aisle, confident that it wouldn't be her. But it is!

She stands there at the entrance, a small bundle of black fur in her arms. Sweat soaks through her cut-off shirt, but all he can focus on is her exposed midriff. He starts walking to her; she hasn't noticed him yet. He sees that she has a belly button piercing; a butterfly charm dangles almost to the top of her jean shorts. The shorts bunch up at the top of her generous thighs; under those are a pair of black fishnets. *Fuck!* Vladimir internally groans, then bites his bottom lip to keep it from falling on the floor.

"You made it," Vladimir says just as she looks up at him. The puppy gives off a little yap then buries his head into her chest. Oh, how he wishes he was that puppy right then.

"Yes, we did! I think he is thirsty. He walked more than halfway here."

"Why don't we go over to the grooming station and get him some water," Vladimir motions for her to follow him, and she does.

When they reach Nelia, she has a big smile on her face, and her hands are clenched at her chest in anticipation.

"This is Tooter. Tooter, this is Nelia. She is going to take a look at you," Vladimir introduces them.

"Tooter," Nelia laughs, "I love it."

"I think he might need some water," Vladimir states.

"Coming right up!" Nelia rushes off to fill a bowl, and Carrisa turns to Vladimir.

"Are you sure this is okay?" She asks.

"Of course, it is. I already told her that you might be coming by, and she was eager to meet him. Between you and me, she had a bad morning, so this actually helps."

"If that's the case, then I don't feel so bad; I didn't want to take advantage," Carrisa admits.

"Not at all. She loves this kind of stuff. Also, we aren't very busy on Mondays," Vladimir assures her.

Nelia returns with a small bowl of water and a couple of soft puppy treats. She sets them down on the grooming table then motions for Carrisa to hand over the puppy. She does so reluctantly. Everyone can tell that the dog loves Carrisa; he whines for a few moments once he leaves her comforting arms.

On the table, Tooter goes right to the bowl and starts lapping up water. "Do you know how old he is?" Nelia asks.

"Um, no. I was hoping you could tell me? I found him by the dumpster in my apartment complex on Friday," Carrisa explains.

"Sounds like a typical dump from a monster some like to call humans." Carrisa nods in agreement as Nelia gives him a good once over. "I am thinking about five weeks. Too young to be away from momma, but he looks good, he will survive. He does have a lot going on in his abdomen, he must be uncomfortable. What is he eating?"

"The Puppy Chow I picked up from here last week," Carrisa answers.

"Okay, I am guessing that he is really gassy, probably has loose stool, and maybe a difficult time pooping. I have some samples that I will give you before you leave. He was taken off the tit too soon, and wasn't given the proper time to wean; not your fault. The stuff I have is soft and mixed in a formula base. He needs to eat this for a couple of weeks before you try the Puppy Chow again."

"Oh, I don't think I will have him in a couple of weeks. I was just keeping him till we found his owner. My boyfriend won't let him stay in the apartment." Carrisa looks ashamed of her situation, but at least she is being honest. Vladimir does not miss the sympathetic smile Nelia slides his way, as if she is in on a secret he doesn't know about.

"Well, wherever he ends up, make sure they get the food I am going to give you. They will also need to take him to the vet to get him de-wormed and get his first set of shots." Nelia is done with her observation and is now giving the puppy one of the treats. "Honestly, I think he has already found his forever home. I don't know what your house is like, but this little guy loves you," Nelia adds while offering Carrisa a smile. "I'll go get those samples for you, be right back."

With Nelia now gone, Tooter rushes over to Carrisa and begs to be picked up. He doesn't have to do much begging. "It's okay little guy; you are going to be okay." Just as she says that, Tooter lets out a righteous fart, and both Vladimir and Carrisa bust out laughing, but that quickly turns into coughing gags due to the smell assaulting their senses.

Holding the bag of free food in one hand and the puppy in the other, Carrisa heads for the door, Vladimir at her side. Once outside, they stop and face each other.

"Thank you so much for this. I know you went above and beyond for me, and I don't know why but I am grateful, and Tooter is grateful also. Maybe I should come up with a better name, but I guess it doesn't matter if I can't keep him," Carrisa snuggles into the puppy, a sad expression on her face. Vladimir knows she wants to keep him but has limited options to offer her.

"How long do you have? I mean, how long did your boyfriend say he could stay?" Vladimir asks.

"Till the end of the week," Carrisa lets out a staggered breath, "Well, actually, he said once the dog food was gone because he wasn't buying anymore, so I guess these cans here have bought Tooter some time," she says with a triumphant smile while holding up the bag.

"That's good," Vladimir states. "Listen, we don't know each other, but I am here if you need any help. I know all the non-kill shelters in and around town, and I might be able to set up a foster home if you need me to do so, but from what I am looking at right now, this is your dog."

"I know, right! It's like we were meant to be together."

"Yes, that's what it feels like," Vladimir adds, not talking about the dog at all. "Anyway, let me give you my number." He pulls a pen and paper out of his back pocket and jots down his number for her. When he hands it over, she is hesitant to take it. "Just in case you need help at the end of the week or when the food runs out," he adds.

She reluctantly takes it and says, "Yes, okay. Just in case I need help finding Tooter a home." She pockets the paper then asks, "So, do you always carry around a pen and paper to hand your number out to girls?"

Vladimir's cheeks heat up at the question. He bows his head then runs a hand down his face before answering,

"Only for the pretty ones that have puppies as cute as this guy here." He laughs at himself; he isn't sure what is wrong with his game right now. He is usually really good at talking to girls, but Carrisa is different. "Sorry, that was a dumb reply. No, I'm the manager, and sometimes I have to take notes on various things, so I always have pen and paper on hand."

"Oh, that's too bad. I liked your first answer better," Carrisa says with a wink. *Is she flirting with me?* Vladimir thinks. *No, she has a live-in boyfriend, a controlling one at that.* "Thanks again Vladimir, I might give you a call, you know, if I need your help." She then turns and walks away.

Vladimir stands there on the sidewalk next to the store entrance long after Carrisa has left his line of vision. Arleen comes up and stands next to him, and he doesn't even notice that she is there until she sparks up a cigarette.

"New girlfriend? Is she the one that added the extra skip in your step earlier today?" Arleen asks.

"No, just a customer," Vladimir replies.

"Oh, I know. I also know that she has a shitty boyfriend, and she should probably leave his ass for you."

"Huh? How in the hell did you get all that out of the little exchange you might have witnessed?" Vladimir thinks this woman must be psychic for a second until it dawns on him. "Oh, yeah, Evette is here; she must have filled you in."

"That she did. Told me all about the adventures you two had on Friday night. I say go for it! If they ain't married, then they are fair game."

"Thanks for your oh-so-moral opinion, but I think I'll pass." Vladimir starts to walk back into the store when Arleen calls to him.

"Hey, you deserve to be happy. Sometimes happiness just falls in our laps. Sometimes we have to chase it, and sometimes we have to fight for it. But there is a reason they call it happiness because no matter how you get it, the destination is worth the journey." *This old bat just might be on to something.*

Chapter Four

That week was a grueling production in Vladimir's eyes. Friday is here, and he never did hear from Carrisa, never saw her again. He didn't want to call her. The ball is in her court. She has his number, and if she needed him for any reason, she would have called—but she hasn't.

Walking into work that day, he offers Arleen a small wave and heads to the back. Lucky for him, she is busy with a customer, so she can't bust his balls like she had been doing every day that week. He isn't in the mood to deal with any of that today. He is in a funk, a fog that he can't seem to get out of at the moment. The good news— tonight is Friday night; he is scheduled off tomorrow so he can drown his sorrows at The Railroad and maybe even grab a rando at last call to take home. Burying himself into some strange sounded about as tempting as sticking his hand into a blender and hitting the puree button, but he is sure once that buzz hits, it won't matter.

Philip meets him at the loading dock out back. They are expecting a shipment this afternoon and need to clear some space for the new inventory.

"Hey man, I hear they got a band at The Railroad tonight, kind of exciting," Philip says as he puts on some gloves then opens the bay door.

"Oh, yeah. Who is it?" Vladimir asks.

"Not sure," Philip shrugs. "Doesn't matter to me, though, better than listening to people trying to sing karaoke."

"That's for damn sure," Vladimir agrees.

The truck arrives, and the two men have it unloaded faster than they ever had. They work together like a finely oiled machine. As soon as they have everything situated and accounted for, Vladimir hears Evette call for him over the loudspeaker.

"Sorry man, gotta go deal with whatever shitshow awaits me up front."

"Better you than me," Philip replies.

Walking up to the front of the store, Vladimir dreads having to deal with a customer. He isn't in the mood to deal with people right now. That is until he sees who is standing by the register. It's Carrisa; she looks distraught and has Tooter in her arms. He struggles like he wants free, wants to run around, but she isn't letting him go just yet.

Vladimir approaches her and asks, "Is everything okay?"

"No," Carrisa says, tears threatening to spill out of her eyes.

"Come here," Vladimir motions for her to follow him to the back office. The place is a mess, and he is ashamed to invite her in, but he feels like she needs some privacy to say what she plans on saying. "What's going on? Is he okay?" Vladimir asks once they are behind closed doors.

"Yeah, I mean everything is not okay, I mean he is okay, I mean he threw up a little but…"

"Slow down, have a seat." Vladimir clears a chair for her, and she takes the offered seat. He then takes the puppy from her hands. Tooter ferociously licks his face, and Vladimir can't help but laugh despite the situation. "He seems to be okay now."

"I know, he is okay. I let him in the house, and he threw up on the carpet, and I didn't see it, but Jalal did, and he got pissed. He said the dog has to go, and I could go with him if I didn't get rid of him today. Can you believe that? How rude!"

"Well, I don't know the dude, but from what I do know, rude does fit the bill." Carrisa just stares at him, mouth agape. "Sorry, I didn't mean that. As I said, I don't know the guy, but he didn't give a great impression when I met him, and considering your state right now, he isn't a great guy. I know he is your boyfriend, but if he threatened to throw you out, what are you doing with him?"

"I don't know. He's all I have. I moved here with him this past summer, and I don't know anyone, and I have no money or family. I depend on him for everything. I don't work, I'm home all day by myself, and I thought Jalal would cave on letting me keep the puppy. But he hasn't, and now I know that he won't; he would rather me leave with Tooter than let me keep him at the apartment." She is crying now, and Vladimir has no idea how to handle this situation.

"Why didn't you call me?"

Carrisa sits rigid, her cheeks heating up instantly. "I'm sorry. I couldn't. Jalal found your number when we were doing laundry, and he got really mad. He isn't a bad guy, but he is kind of protective, and he doesn't want me talking to other guys."

"Other guys or other people? I was just trying to help with the dog. I wasn't asking you out. I knew you had a boyfriend. Do you need me to explain this to him?" Vladimir asks, wholly disturbed by Carrisa's admissions.

"I don't think that will help, but thanks. I could use your help with Tooter now. Is your offer still available? I can't just abandon him; I love him, and he loves me. I can't let him go now. I know it sounds stupid."

Vladimir stops her there, "That does not sound stupid. If anyone gets what you are saying, it's me. If you could see my apartment, then you would understand."

"You have pets?" Carrisa asks.

"Um, I am the manager of a pet store, where I've worked since I was sixteen. Yes, I have pets. Not this kind," he stops and points to Tooter, "but pets all the same. And pets that I think of as family."

"What kind of pets do you have?"

"Well, I have reptiles, so my pets mainly stay contained. Although, I do have a Boa Constrictor that currently roams free, and he eats whole chickens. He would try to eat Tooter here; I am sure of it," Vladimir adds.

Carrisa's eyes widen. "I love snakes. I've never had one, but I had a best friend in high school that had one and used to feed him mice. They are so cool and beautiful," Carrisa has a dreamy expression as she says this, and Vladimir can feel his pants tightening. He tries to calm himself before she notices, as now is definitely not an appropriate time for his ever-growing affections to show.

"How old are you?" Vladimir asks. "Sorry, that was a rude question."

"Oh, no, that's okay. I'm nineteen; I graduated high school last year. I'm from Dallas, but Jalal got this job over here, so I decided to move with him. He promised to take care of me, and that he does, but it's not what I thought it would be. I haven't been here long, but I thought I would have a job and maybe a couple of friends by now. I'm sorry, you don't want to hear all of this. Look, can you help me with Tooter? I would really appreciate it."

"Yes, but do you need help with Tooter, or do you need help with you know… you?" Vladimir is hesitant with his question, but he knows that it needs to be asked. If he learned anything from what happened with his family a couple of years ago, it was to ask more questions.

Carrisa looks around the small room, unsure of how to answer that, "Um, I don't really know what to say to that question. Right now, as in right at this moment, I need help with the dog. You said you could help. Can you, or can't you?"

"I tell you what. How about I take him for the weekend. This will give you some time to smooth things over at home. If we hand him over to a shelter or a foster home, he is gone; you won't be able to get him back because that would be you surrendering the dog. We both know that this dog belongs to you, and you belong to him. How about you leave him with me and talk to Jalal. Maybe if the dog is out of the picture for a little bit and he sees how unhappy you are, he might change his mind."

Carrisa shakes her head but then slowly changes it to a nod, "That might not be a bad idea. That might actually work. But wait, where would you keep him? You already said that your snake will try to eat him."

Vladimir sets Tooter down; the dog starts to sniff around, and the two watch him for a minute before Vladimir speaks again, "Topsy basically stays in the living room, more specifically under the couch. He is also completely harmless and only eats about once a month. I just fed him four days ago, so he won't mess with Tooter here. But to be safe, I will keep him with me. I'll let him sleep with me in the bedroom and shut Topsy out."

"You are going to let him sleep with you, like in your bed?" Carrisa asks with a bewildered expression.

"Yeah, where else would he sleep? I don't have a yard, but we can go for walks. I'm off tomorrow, and it will be fun. I never had a dog growing up. Never had any pets besides snakes and lizards. I have a little brother who is allergic to everything with fur, so this will be an adventure for both of us, a cool sleepover."

Carrisa stands up and collects Tooter before he can pee on something. "This is so great. You have no idea how much this means to me. I better get home; Jalal will be there soon and wonder where I am if I'm not back before he is. Can I leave him now, while you're at work?"

"Yeah, it's cool. He can hang with me until I get off. Pets are always welcome in here." Vladimir suddenly remembers that he is supposed to go out with the crew after work, but he will have to miss out tonight. He doesn't want to let Carrisa and Tooter down right after offering to take him.

"Okay, well, when do you work next?" Carrisa inquires.

"Sunday, I have the late shift, noon to six. I'll bring him with me, so either call or come by to let me know what's up, okay?"

"You got it; I will. And thanks again." She gives Tooter a kiss before handing him over and walking out of the small office.

Vladimir follows a few feet behind her but keeps his distance. He allows her to exit without another word. He waits a few minutes then heads outside to set the puppy down on a patch of grass so he can relieve himself. The puppy takes care of business, and by the time they round the corner, Carrisa is nowhere in sight.

Chapter Five

When Vladimir gets home, he tries to introduce Topsy and Tooter to each other. Tooter is scared to death of the snake, and Topsy wants absolutely nothing to do with the puppy. He had picked up a few essentials from the store before he left: a dog bed, some food, a couple of toys, a leash with a matching collar; he even made him a tag in the engraving machine that says 'Tooter'.

The puppy is full of excitement as he explores his new surroundings. Vladimir even leaves the door open as he showers, and Tooter climbs in and sits under the spray. He doesn't have any dog shampoo, but Vladimir doesn't think the little guy cares.

The two of them eat dinner in the bedroom while watching late-night television until they can't keep their eyes open. He doesn't hear from Carissa, but he hadn't expected a call. She said she no longer had his number, and the only way she could reach him was through work. Vladimir hoped she was okay. He hoped Jalal hadn't given her any shit and that maybe he was starting to give in to the idea of letting her keep the dog.

The next day Vladimir is woken up long before he had planned by a little puppy tongue lapping at his nose. Tooter was a good pup. He hadn't had an accident in the house, not once, and he even let Vladimir sleep until the sun came up. Still, he could have used a few more hours considering that it was his day off, but he is glad to take his new four-legged friend out for a walk at the crack of dawn.

When they come back into the apartment, Vladimir has a message on his machine. It is from Stewart, and he wants to know why he hadn't shown up at The Railroad the night before. Now that Vladimir knows his best friend is awake, he decides to call him back.

"Hey," Stewart says into the phone.

"Hey, man. You are up early," Vladimir states.

"What happened to you last night? Philip said you just went home, saying you had something to take care of and left work with a damn puppy in your arms."

"Yeah, man. Sorry I didn't get a chance to page you and let you know I wouldn't be there. Something came up," Vladimir let out, ready for the inquisition.

"Something, as in a puppy? You never struck me as the kind of dude to want a dog. Was he food for Topsy?" Stewart laughs.

Vladimir lets out a breath then says, "No, man. There's this girl, well, this customer actually. She found it at her apartment complex, and she wants to keep it, so I said I would basically babysit him for the weekend."

"Oh, Shit! Vlad gots some deep ass puppy love thing going on."

"It's not like that," Vladimir says a little defensively.

"Yeah, right," Stewart draws out his words in disbelief. "I have never, in all these years, I have never seen you do a chick a favor unless there is something in it for you."

"Well, I have to admit that she is cute as fuck, but she has this asshole boyfriend, so I'm not going to even go there," Vladimir shakes his head even though his friend can't see him. "I don't need that kind of drama in my life."

"Oh, we all need a little drama sometimes. What fun is life if you don't stir the shit pot every now and again," Stewart teases. "Anyway, we will get back to that later. Did you know that Elan showed up last night and brought some fine ass chick with him?"

"Oh, man, he did show. I feel bad now. I was giving him shit about not hanging out with us, and then he does, and I'm not even there. Was it Addy?" Vladimir asks.

"Yeah, you remember her. She is fucking hot; I remember getting a hard-on every time I passed her in the hall back in the day. I never got to talk to her back then because, well, she was way out of any of our leagues. Hell, she is cool as shit. A little shy but funny when she gets a couple of drinks in her. Elan was lost, dude; he has fucking lost it for this girl. He waited on her hand and foot last night, anything she wanted." Vladimir is disappointed that he missed out on seeing that but is also happy for his big brother.

"I know who she is, but I just recently found out that they were dating. Y'all didn't give him any shit last night, did you?" Vladimir hopes they didn't make Elan and his new girl feel uncomfortable. If they did, then he wouldn't be bringing her up to The Railroad again anytime soon. Elan was weird like that.

"Give Elan shit? Hell no! I am pretty sure everyone knows not to fuck with his ass."

"Cool, maybe I'll get to see them next Friday," Vladimir states.

"Yeah, like at their wedding. Those two looked like the real deal." Vladimir hopes so, Elan has been a wreck since Trish, and he needs someone to help him move on with his life. "Say, man, what are you up to today?"

"Same thing as every Saturday, cleaning atriums and doing laundry," Vladimir answers in a cheerful tone. "Only now I got a little buddy to help out."

"I don't think that dog is going to help you much," Stewart remarks. "Is it cool if I come by for a bit, say in like an hour?"

"Yeah, of course," Vladimir replies.

They end their call, and Vladimir realizes that Tooter is in desperate need of water after their walk. He fills the bowl and adds an ice cube; he can't drink water without ice, so figures the pup would enjoy it. All the ice does is make Tooter growl at it, then try to fish it from the bowl and cause a huge mess on the floor. Vladimir doesn't care, and he has fun watching the little pup make the mess.

He doesn't understand why Stewart constantly asks if he can come over; the man comes over every Saturday. They don't do much, just watch TV, maybe play some PlayStation, but it is nice having someone over. When he had offered his brothers the roommate position, he didn't really want a roommate but figured it was the right thing to do at the time. However, at quiet times like these, he does miss having someone around—the loneliness would sink in deep; he assumed it was from being part of a large family and never having a moment alone before.

Now that it has been almost a year since he moved out on his own, he figures he either needs to find a steady girlfriend or look for a legit roommate—shit or get off the pot. This thought has been running circles in his mind for a couple of months now. Since it isn't going anywhere, he assumes it is trying to tell him something.

At only twenty-two, he has plenty of time to make life decisions, but like his mother is always reminding him, he isn't getting any younger.

When Stewart arrives, they heat up some Hot Pockets and play Street Fighter for a couple of hours. Tooter starts to whine after a long nap in Vladimir's lap, so he figures the little dude is ready for another walk.

During the walk, Stewart asks, "So, what are you going to do with him when you have to work? You know you can't just leave a puppy at home alone for eight to ten hours at a time. These guys need constant attention when they are this little. What is he anyway?"

"I know this man! He's a dog," Vladimir exclaims. "I said it was only for the weekend. I have to work tomorrow, and I plan on taking him with me. Carrisa is supposed to come by and let me know what's up. If she can't keep him, then I was thinking of hosting an adoption-type thing in the store. Some of those big-name stores do it, so I guess I have to think about it just in case."

"So, she has a name," Stewart teases. "Carrisa, I like it. What's she like?"

"Like nothing else," comes Vladimir's wistful reply.

"Oh, shit, we're in trouble now. That bad, huh?" Stewart asks.

"I can't think about it like that. She has a boyfriend, and like I said, that shit ain't for me. I am just going to help her with the dog here, and if she doesn't keep it, I will probably never see her again."

"In Tyler? You think you can just avoid people in this small ass town? Never going to happen, you will see her again, no matter what."

"Look, she isn't even from here. She just moved here with her boyfriend from Dallas. From the sound of it, things aren't that great, so if they don't work out, then she will probably hightail it back to Dallas," Vladimir says.

"Unless she has another reason to stay," Stewart remarks.

"I am no Captain Save-A-Hoe!"

"We all say that until there is a hoe worth saving," Stewart rebukes.

Vladimir rolls his eyes then says, "Whatever, let's get back inside so I can whip your ass in Street Fighter again."

Chapter Six

Vladimir and Tooter had a lot of fun together on Saturday. When Sunday morning rolls around, Vladimir takes him for a long walk then sets him up in the bathroom. He thinks it might not be best to bring him to the store for his entire shift. He is usually pretty busy on Sundays, considering he has every Saturday off. He will come back during his break at three to pick the little guy up, but with water, food, and some newspaper to pee on, Tooter should be okay till then.

Once he sets foot into Pet Palace, he is glad he made the decision to leave Tooter at home. The place is packed, thanks to their fall sale that Vladimir had completely forgotten about. Evette and the new hire, Tag, are both working the registers and the lines are still five deep. The store only has two registers, but Vladimir jumps in to take Tag's spot to speed things up before doing anything else. It wasn't an insult to Tag; he is just new, so in turn, he is slow.

Time flies by, and once Vladimir has a moment to breathe, it is already ten past three. He hadn't thought about it being this busy and not being able to leave and check on the puppy. Just when he is about to make his escape, a disheveled Carrisa enters the doors carrying a loaded backpack on her back.

Vladimir almost runs into her as he tries to exit. "Hey there, are you okay?" Vladimir asks, taking note of her puffy eyes and worried expression.

"Oh, yeah. I'm glad I caught you. Sorry I didn't come back sooner, but I had some stuff to deal with. Do you have a minute?" Carrisa asks.

"Yeah. Oh, wait. Hey, so I left Tooter at my apartment, and I was just about to go check on him. Um, do you want to come with? I just live around the corner, and I promise I'm not some serial killer or anything like that. We can talk on the way, and I'll even let you hold a knife to me the entire time if that makes you more comfortable." Carrisa's eyes widen at Vladimir's words.

"Wow, I'm not usually that paranoid, but now that you have laid it all out there, I am thinking of upping my game. Sure, I can't wait to see him; I actually could use some puppy love right about now." Vladimir is reminded of what Stewart had said to him yesterday. How he had a little puppy love going on. Now that he is face to face with Carrisa again, his friend might not have been too far off in his assessment.

"This way." Vladimir walks Carrisa to his car and opens the door for her. She doesn't say anything about the gesture, but her body language says enough. She isn't used to men acting like gentlemen, and even though Vladimir may be a player at times, his father's values are deeply ingrained.

They arrive at his apartment complex, and once again, he opens the door for her and helps her out, giant backpack and all. After opening his door, he allows her to enter first, and she stops right past the threshold and just looks around.

"Sorry, I know it is dark and looks a little creepy in here, but that's just for the snake's benefit. I would leave the door open for you so you can feel safer, but Topsy might get out."

"Oh, shit!" Carrisa visibly recoils and stiffens up. "I forgot you had an anaconda in this bitch. He won't eat me, will he?"

"No, not that kind of snake. Come on; I locked Tooter in the bathroom so he wouldn't get eaten while I was at work because I am sorry to say this, but Topsy is THAT kind of snake."

"This place is badass, and I want to look around some more, but I need some puppy in my life first," Carrisa announces.

"This way, the bathroom is in my bedroom, and again, I will not try anything; I will even stay a few feet behind you."

Carrisa heads into the bedroom; then, before opening the bathroom door, she turns to Vladimir and says,

"Okay, we are going to revisit your paranoia issues after I get my puppy kisses." With that, she opens the bathroom door, and whatever Vladimir was going to say is forgotten. Tooter comes rushing out and jumps into Carrisa's crouched frame. Vladimir is lost in the sight of the two of them before the smell hits him. Tooter had done more than toot over the last few hours. He had made a mess of the bathroom. Shit and piss are everywhere, and none of it is on the newspaper Vladimir had set out. The newspaper is torn to shreds, his food and water dish are toppled over, and most of it is mixed in with the piss and shit.

"I'm sorry, this is not how my house normally looks," Vladimir apologizes.

Carrisa looks up from kissing the puppy then glances around. "Oh, yeah. This is about how my balcony looked last week. I get it, he sure can make a big mess for such a little fellow."

"Yeah, I see that now," Vladimir replies.

" I can clean it up. Thank you so much for taking care of him. I just can't seem to say goodbye to this little guy." Carrisa snuggles back into the ball of black fur, at the same time, Tooter looks up at Vladimir with the saddest expression, like he is begging both of them not to let him go, not to abandon him like his previous owners.

Carrisa stands, Tooter tightly tucked into her arms. "Okay, let's get him outside so he can run around for a minute."

The two of them head back outside and let Tooter run free in the courtyard. Vladimir checks the time on his watch. He still has fifteen minutes, but he should probably let Carrisa know that he needs to get back, and at the same time ask her what her plan is, you know, with the dog.

"So, I do have to head back to work in a few minutes. No rush, just wanted to let you know."

"Okay, so you are not getting off that easy;. What is up with you, and your need to make me feel comfortable? Either someone has accused you of something before, or you are actually a rapist or killer and are trying to throw me off track."

"Nothing like that. Something happened to one of my sisters not that long ago, and I always want females to feel comfortable around me. If you ever feel uncomfortable or like you need to get away, I don't want to get in the way. I am here to help. My baby sister went through some shit, and I never want to see what I saw in her in anyone, not even a stranger," Vladimir admits.

"Well, we definitely need to delve deeper into this, but as you said, you only have a few minutes, and I don't think a few minutes is going to cover it," Carrisa looks over at him with a smile, her bleached pixie hair glistening in the sun.

"First off, what is up with the bag?" Vladimir asks as he points to the backpack still strapped to Carrisa's back.

"Oh, you noticed that, huh?"

"You going somewhere?" Vladimir inquires.

"Well, yeah, I guess. I don't really know, and I'm sure you don't want to hear about it," Carrisa sighs then shakes her head before she continues. "I have some shit to figure out, and it is a lot to relay. I don't think we have the time for that right now. Short story, I am not going back to my apartment with Jalal. I came here to collect my dog then hop on a Greyhound to Dallas. The only thing is, I don't know where to go from there."

"You left him?" Vladimir is ecstatic and trying his hardest not to let it show.

"I did, but truth be told, there is more to it than just that. Right now, I'm sure you don't want to hear my sob story. You have to get back to work, and I don't want to keep you."

"When does your bus leave?" Vladimir asks.

Carrisa shakes her head in shame. "I have to get to the station first. They have a western union there. I'm going to try and reach my mom and see if she can wire me the funds to get a ticket, then I'll know."

"So, you don't have much of a plan. Sorry, you have a plan, but it sounds to me like you are reliant on your mother answering a call and sending you money for it to see fruition. Is there a possibility that she won't?"

"There is a strong possibility, but I'll figure it out. As long as we can get to Dallas, Tooter and I can stay with either my mom, my aunt, or my sister. Either which way, it will work out. It has to." The look in Carissa's eyes rings anything but hope. She doesn't even believe her own words, and Vladimir sees that.

"Okay," Vladimir finally says, "I have to get back to work, but I do not feel comfortable letting you walk to the bus station without knowing what is going to happen once you get there. How about this. I will let you stay here while I finish my shift. While I am gone, you can use my phone to call whoever you need to call and secure an actual travel plan. Does that sound okay to you?"

"Really? You don't even know me, and you're gonna let me stay in your house and use your phone?" Carrisa asks, skepticism written all over her face.

"Remember, I have Topsy to protect me. He may be docile, but given one command, he will attack!" Vladimir proclaims.

"Really? I thought you said he wasn't that kind of snake?"

"Sorry, that was just me trying to be assertive. He won't do anything, but for real, though, either stay outside with Tooter and keep the door closed or stay in my room. We don't need him wandering around," Vladimir admits.

"Okay, thank you. This actually helps a lot. I can try to reach my family and get them to send me some funds because I think Western Union takes a little while to go through. I will be out of your hair in no time." Vladimir doesn't know if he wants her out of his hair. He likes having Tooter around, and having Carrisa would be way more fun, especially considering that she finally broke things off with Jalal.

"So, stay here. I have to head back to work, but I will be back before seven. There is food in the kitchen. Don't be scared to go in there; as I said, Topsy already ate this month and will stay under the couch as long as she is not disturbed. Are you okay with that?" Vladimir asks in a rush.

"Wow! That sounds stellar. I think I can manage that. Thank you for trusting me to stay in your home without you," Carrisa says.

Vladimir arrives back at Pet Palace a few minutes late. Evette gives him a hurry-up look as soon as he enters. He was supposed to relieve her for her last fifteen-minute break, and the teen isn't keen on missing it.

"Sorry," Vladimir apologizes and moves in to ring up the next customer for Evette.

Evette rolls her eyes and mumbles, "I'm taking my full fifteen."

"Of course, have a blast," Vladimir says before turning back to the customer.

The store settles down a little after five, and Tag, Evette, and Vladimir start doing closing chores so they can get out of there right after six. Ten minutes before six, the bell chimes at the entryway. Vladimir is in the back cleaning up a toppled-over dog food pallet when he hears a commotion.

"Where the fuck is that goth dude that works here?" Someone yells, and Vladimir can hear every word as he rushes up front to save his employees from being attacked.

As Vladimir comes around the corner, he sees an irate-looking Jalal standing by the first register. The boy is a little smaller than Vladimir, and he is sure he could take him if things get out of hand, but he hopes that it won't come to that. Vladimir might not be athletic like the other Frazier men, but he carries the same build. The only activity he ever partakes in is hiking, but that is enough to keep him in shape.

"Can I help you?" Vladimir asks calmly. He knows why Jalal is here, but Vladimir intends on playing dumb with this fool.

"You can't help me, but you can help yourself," Jalal yells into Vladimir's face while stepping into his personal space and pointing a finger into his tight chest. "Where the fuck is my girlfriend?"

"You are going to have to narrow that down for me, sir. Who is this girlfriend you speak of?" Vladimir asks with a cocky smirk.

"Oh, you want to play games, funny man," Jalal's face starts to heat up as he bucks to Vladimir, indicating that he is ready for a fight. "Carrisa, you dip shit. I know you were putting the moves on her. She tossed your number, but you somehow found a way to reach her anyway. She told me you were the one holding that damn dog for her like you were doing her a favor. We all know you just want to get in her pants, but that shit is not going to happen. Not now and not ever! She belongs to me, and she needs to get her ass back home, so where are you hiding her?"

Vladimir lets out a sarcastic laugh as if this is all a game to him, "Sounds to me like she left your ass. Also, why would she need to hide? Should she be scared or something?"

"That's it!" Jalal cocks his fist back and lands a hard blow right into Vladimir's cheek. Tag and Evette both let out frightened gasps, but Vladimir just shakes his head and laughs once again.

Before Vladimir reacts, he silently tells himself to keep his calm, he is at work, and no matter what this fucker does, Vladimir will suffer consequences if he retaliates. "All right, I am going to let you have that one since you seem to be pretty upset, but that's the only free pass you are ever going to get from me." He grips his hands together in front of him in an attempt to keep them at bay and also make it look as if he has some control over the situation. "Now, let's try this again. Your supposed girlfriend obviously doesn't want to be found, or as you put it, she wouldn't be hiding from you."

Jalal fumes and then comes charging in Vladimir's direction as if he is a linebacker and they are on a football field. Vladimir sidesteps out of the way just in time, and Jalal tumbles to the floor, his face squeaking as it slides along the polished linoleum.

"Alright, that's enough. This is a place of business, and we have work to do." Before Jalal can stand, Vladimir grabs him by the back collar, lifts him up, then drags him to the front doors. He tosses the asshole out on his ass and says, "Get going before I call the fucking cops." Vladimir then locks the doors so everyone can close up for the evening. "Alright, y'all close your tills so we can get the hell out of here." Evette and Tag are speechless but shake it off quickly when they see that Vladimir isn't playing around.

Twenty-five minutes later, the three Pet Palace employees exit the store and enter an almost empty parking lot. Looks like Jalal listened to the threat and left. There is no sign of him anywhere, or so Vladimir thought.

Chapter Seven

When Vladimir arrives home a few minutes later, he finds Tooter and Carrisa on the back porch playing tug-of-war with one of the rope toys. He hadn't checked his reflection, but he could feel swelling starting to form in his left cheek. Little troll packed a mean punch, and Vladimir is sure there would be a bruise by morning.

Apparently, it was already forming because that's the first thing Carrisa notices, "What happened to your face?"

"What? Nothing, what is it?"

"By your mouth, it's all puffy and red." Carrisa moves in to get a better look, but Vladimir shies away.

"Nothing," Vladimir holds a hand up to block her view. He thought about lying, about not telling her he got a visit from Jalal, but that would be stupid, and he didn't think it was right to keep it from her. "Jalal came by the store right before we closed. He is a great guy. I see why you picked him," he says sarcastically.

"No," Carrisa covers her mouth, shame is written all over her face. "I am so sorry. He hit you, didn't he? You have been nothing but nice to me and all I do is bring drama everywhere I go. I am sorry, I'll get out of your hair, and you shouldn't have to deal with him anymore. Once he knows I am not with you, he will leave you alone. Trust me, his bark is bigger than his bite."

"I don't know about that; his bite was pretty impressive. Took a lot for me not to hit him back. I just had to remind myself that he wasn't worth losing my job over," Vladimir admits. However, he knows that if the asshole tries something again, he won't be getting off so easily next time.

"Sorry, let me just gather Tooter, and 'we'll go."

"Where are you going? Did you get a hold of your family?" Vladimir asks as they move inside. "I have to change and head over to my parents' house for dinner, but I can drop you at the bus station on the way."

"No, my mom doesn't have a home phone, so I left a message for her at her work. She wasn't there, and I didn't know your number, so she doesn't have a way to call me back, but I'll try her and my sister again at the bus station." Carrisa looks ashamed to admit all her shortcomings, but he doesn't fault her for them. We can't do anything about where we come from; he learned that all too well from Trent Lockley.

"No, that's not going to work. I'm not going to just drop you off with no plan. Let me call my mom really quick, and you can come have dinner with us," Vladimir says.

"Are you sure?" Carrisa sounds hesitant but hopeful.

"Oh, yeah. My mom lives for guests."

Vladimir calls his mother while he changes and tells her he has two guests joining him but that only one will be eating, so she only needs to set one extra setting at the table. He also tells her that Peter might want to drop an antihistamine now; otherwise, he will be hurting later. This made his mother snicker as she realized a pet would be entering their home, and everyone was going to either freak out or have a joyous fit.

The three of them head over to the Frazier home. Carrisa is unsure what she will be walking into but is happy to have a home-cooked meal for once. She and Jalal lived off of fast food and mac and cheese. He rarely bought anything for her to cook even though she has told him a million times that she loves cooking.

Being the last to arrive for dinner, Vladimir sees that Elan has also brought a guest. Addy is here, in his living room, sitting on the sofa and having a one-on-one discussion with his father. Michael is a man of few words, and seeing his face light up at whatever Addy had just said is refreshing.

As soon as Vladimir sets Tooter down, Hannah comes running, ready to attack.

"A puppy!" The little girl yells.

"Be careful with him, Hannah. He is just a baby," Vladimir softly says to his niece. "You need to treat him like you do with Stephan."

"That thing better not pee on my carpet," Mary Beth chastises, but the smile on her face says she wouldn't care if he did.

"This is why I had to take a Benadryl? Okay, I guess being drowsy all night is worth it," Peter moves in to get a better look as he says this.

Everyone is so enthralled by the puppy that they don't even notice Carrisa standing there. She awkwardly waits in the entry hall for instructions on what to do next. Vladimir notices her and motions for her to come on inside the living room. She moves hesitantly, and Peter is the first one to greet her.

"Hi, I'm Peter, Vlad's younger brother," he introduces himself as he leans in and reaches out a hand.

She shakes his hand and, with a nod, says, "Hi, I am Carrisa, Vladimir's, uh, friend, I guess." Vladimir gives her a warm smile. He likes that she can call him a friend. Of course, after everything he has done for her in the past few days, he could consider himself an exceptionally good friend indeed.

"And where have you been hiding her?" Mary Beth asks.

"Nowhere, Mom, we just met," Vladimir admits.

"Well, any friend of Vlad's is welcome here. Come on in, dear. We are just getting ready to sit down." Mary Beth takes Carrisa's hand and leads her to the dining room; everyone else follows. "Hannah, go wash up, you have puppy hair all over your hands," Mary Beth states, and the girl pouts but does as she is told.

Carrisa and Addy sit next to each other. This gives them comfort as they are both newcomers to the Frazier home. Introductions are made, and plates are passed around. Once everyone's bellies are full, Mary Beth starts a pot of decaf coffee, and almost everyone else heads outside to follow Tooter around.

"Why do you call him Tooter?" Hannah asks.

"Well, because he likes to toot," Carrisa laughs, and everyone joins in. "Well, not so much anymore, I guess, but he did when I first found him."

"I like it, but if you are going to change it, you should call him Midnight," Elan pipes in from where he stands next to Addy.

"Why's that?" Vladimir asks.

"Because he is black as midnight, duh," Elan shakes his head as if that was obvious.

"No, that's too basic. He needs an original name, it should stay Tooter," Peter says.

The family enjoys their coffee out back as the dog runs around. Thomas and Nigel are the first to leave. Phoebe and Mark have to practically drag a screaming Hannah out the door. She refuses to leave Tooter, and Phoebe is not so subtle in her disdain for what Vladimir has done. Now she just might have to get the girl a dog of her own. With a toddler and a newborn, that was not something Phoebe had a desire to do.

Vladimir and Carrisa head out right before ten. The only people left are the ones that live there, plus Addy.

On their way back to Vladimir's apartment, Carrisa breaks the silence, "So, I guess you can take us to the station now."

"Oh, shit. I don't think that would be a good idea, pretty sure the last bus leaves before ten. You also need to get a hold of your mom, and we should call the automated line and check the bus schedule for tomorrow. I don't have to be at work until noon tomorrow, so I can stay up with you for a bit. That is, if you want." Vladimir wasn't sure what he was thinking, keeping her from taking care of responsibilities all night. If he would have just dropped her off earlier like she asked, then she would already be in Dallas.

"Okay, but I don't know where I would go after that. I can't go back to Jalal this late; he might not let me in."

"If that's the same guy I saw earlier, then he is going to be waiting up for you." Vladimir laughs, but it dies down quickly when Carrisa doesn't join in. "For real, though, what is up with that guy?"

"Well, I did kind of storm out after a big fight earlier, so he probably isn't in the best place." Carrisa lets out a long sigh, then says, "Look, I know you don't need to hear all my drama but just a warning: Jalal has a temper, and he is really possessive."

"I have gathered that much on my own."

"For a while now, it's just been him and me. I know this is stupid to say, but I think he felt threatened by Tooter here." She looks down at the puppy currently sleeping on her lap. "I don't know what he's capable of, but I've seen him do some crazy shit when rage takes over him."

"Well, I have dealt with my fair share of crazy in the past. If you feel comfortable enough you can always stay at my place for a bit. I'll take the couch and spend some quality time with Topsy," Vladimir offers.

"I couldn't do that," Carrisa hangs her head as she replies.

Vladimir reaches over and lifts her chin with two fingers. "I would find it offensive if you didn't. I promise to be nothing but a perfect gentleman."

"Oh, I don't doubt that you would. Your family is incredible, by the way. I wish I had one like that," Carrisa looks at him with a small smile on her face.

Vladimir parks, and before getting out, he says, "So it's settled. You can try to reach your mom and sister tonight, and if you don't, no big deal. You can try again in the morning."

Vladimir helps her and Tooter out of the passenger seat and then grabs the bag of leftovers his mother insisted that he take out of the back seat. It's dark; the lightpost by his building has been out for months now. Until now, it hasn't bothered Vladimir at all. Just as Vladimir puts the key in his lock, someone shouts from a dark corner.

"Carrisa!" Comes Jalal's angry voice. They can't see him, but Carrisa's entire body shakes as soon as she hears her name, and Tooter lets out an indignant cry. She knows that voice, and she knows that call all too well.

Tooter starts barking as ferociously as his little frame can when Jalal steps out of the shadows. He is holding a baseball bat in one hand; it swings lazily at his side with each step. "So, you did come here, you cheating fucking bitch!" Jalal seethes.

"Hey, that's no way to talk to a lady," Vladimir says, stepping between him and Carrisa, tossing the bag of leftovers against the wall and ready for a fight.

"This is none of your fucking business. Once I am done with you, you won't have any business at all!" Jalal moves in closer and swings the bat up, letting it land on his shoulder. He now grips it with both hands.

"You have this all wrong," Vladimir says while holding up his empty hands. He looks back at Carrisa for just a second. "Go inside."

She is frozen and doesn't seem to hear Vladimir's request. "Don't you fucking dare. You are coming back home with me. Look, you can even bring the dog with you, but if this fucker has laid his hands on you, he has to pay." That's when he swings.

The bat comes flying towards Vladimir's face, but he is quick and grabs it before Jalal can meet his mark. It stings—bad, in his hands—but Vladimir doesn't let that slow him down. He yanks the bat from a startled Jalal's arms and tosses it to the side. The sound of it bouncing off the concrete ground echoes all around them. Now, Vladimir is pissed. He isn't at work, so nothing gets held back.

Before anyone knows what is happening, Vladimir has Jalal by the shirt and against the wall. He slams the smaller man up against the stucco with as much force as he can gather.

"You always come to people's homes and treat them this way? No, fuck that. Do you always talk to her like that?" Vladimir spits into Jalal's face as he speaks between clenched teeth. "No wonder she left your ass."

Jalal seems to gather himself just then and starts to grab at Vladimir, trying and failing to push him away. He does, however, manage to scratch at Vladimir's neck, breaking the skin and causing it to burn. Vladimir steps back, only enough to give him the space to land a powerful fist right into Jalal's nose. His head bounces off the wall, and blood pours from his nostrils. Somewhere behind him, he faintly hears a scream coming from Carrisa. Jalal swings with both arms going for anything he can get. He manages to catch a couple of blows to Vladimir's chest and chin before he is thrown onto his back. Vladimir is on him that instant.

All bets are off; this fucker came to his house looking for a fight, and that is just what he will get. Vladimir holds nothing back as he plummets into Jalal's face over and over again. The upstairs neighbor comes out, looks over the stair railing, and calls down to them, begging them to stop and stating that he has called the police.

"Vlad, stop. That's enough!" Carrisa shouts for the hundredth time, but it finally gets through.

Vladimir looks down at Jalal, seeing the destruction he has caused. His fist is covered in blood. Jalal is coughing up blood, and a tooth fragment hits the concrete. It is so quiet now that they can hear it land in the puddle under Jalal. Sirens start to wail in the distance.

"Fuck, Fuck. FUCK!" Vladimir screams, then stands up. Jalal is conscious, but his face is unrecognizable.

"Is he..." Carrisa's words fade off as a squad car comes to a skidding halt just fifteen feet away from them. Two officers jump out and rush to them with guns aimed in Vladimir's direction.

"Down on the ground!" One of the officers says, and Vladimir realizes that this command is being directed at him.

Vladimir does not hesitate. He has never been arrested before, but he knows the drill. With his back still towards the officers, he holds up both arms, then kneels onto the ground and places his palms behind his head. The officer that cuffs him isn't gentle, and it's almost like he enjoys being rough.

Vladimir is not read his rights, and he takes that as a sign that he isn't actually being arrested at this moment, just detained.

"Take my keys and either go inside like I said before or take my car to meet me at the station," Vladimir calmly says to Carrisa without even looking in her direction.

He is hauled off in the squad car after an ambulance arrives. He isn't sure if Carrisa is going to join him or choose to help her shitty ass boyfriend.

Chapter Eight

Vladimir is taken to the police station and left in a holding cell for almost an hour before anyone even tries to talk to him. He wasn't given the option to wash up and hasn't been asked for his side of the story yet. He has no idea what happened with Jalal or Carrisa, but he doesn't care at this point. No one even asked if he needed to call anyone—not his parents or a lawyer.

The officer that cuffed him approaches the cell door. "Alright, Mohamed Ali, let's do this."

"What are we going to do?" Vladimir asks once he is cuffed again and pushed down a dim hallway.

"I need to take your statement," the officer says.

Vladimir is left in an interrogation room alone for only a few minutes before the officer returns with a cup of water. He offers it to Vladimir, then takes a seat across the table and sets down a pad of paper and a pen.

"Okay, let's get started."

"Is Jalal alright?" Vladimir asks.

"Do you really care?" The officer inquires. Vladimir nods his head, so the officer releases a breath and says, "He is going to be okay. You really did a number on him, but I can't say he didn't deserve it. They took him to the hospital. My partner is there and will be arresting him as soon as he is released."

"What do you mean, he deserved it?" He was sure Jalal didn't tell the whole truth about what went down.

"Well, first off, your neighbor saw the whole thing go down, the one that called us. Between his statement and what Carrisa Abbot has given us, we know that it was self-defense. It was excessive, I will give you that, but after talking with Carrisa and seeing the marks, I can't say I wouldn't have done the same thing."

Vladimir didn't know what he was talking about when he said marks. What marks? He thought it best not to say anything as that might jeopardize his freedom, so he just nodded along.

"Look, it has been a long night. I need you to write down everything that happened tonight. Also, include what happened before that might have led up to this guy meeting you at your door with a bat. I'll give you a little while to do this, and then you are free to go." The officer then moves to remove the cuffs from Vladimir's wrists. "Sorry, just a precaution. Sometimes rage takes people over, and they take it out on us. Am I safe to remove these?" Vladimir just gives another nod.

Once the officer is gone, Vladimir picks up the pen and starts writing. He begins with his first interaction with Jalal and Carrisa over a week ago, then moves on to earlier that day at Pet Palace. He also lists the names of his co-workers in case they want to corroborate his story. He is only halfway done with the activity that led him to his current location when the officer pokes his head in. Vladimir holds up a finger, indicating that he needs another minute.

When he is finished, the officer escorts him to the front of the station, and Vladimir is free to go. He assumes that he gets to walk home since no one offers him a ride. Glancing at the clock in the lobby, he sees that it is already after midnight, and he wouldn't dare call anyone to come pick him up. First off, he doesn't want to disturb them, but he also doesn't want them all up in his business.

Walking out to the parking lot with his head hanging low, he starts for the street when he hears Carrisa call to him, "You need a lift?"

"You are here," Vladimir says in astonishment. He had not expected to ever see her again.

"Of course, I am," Carrisa laughs lightly. "You said to use your car, so I did. I put Tooter in your bathroom. I hope that is okay. I just didn't know how long we would be and if they would let me bring him inside."

Vladimir takes the keys that Carrisa holds out to him, his hands still covered in dry blood. He then moves in to hug her and says into her hair once she returns the hug, "Thank you."

"My pleasure."

They drive back to his apartment, both too exhausted to talk about what had happened. Vladimir is full of questions, but he figures they could wait till morning. He had gone through hell today, and all he wants right now is sleep.

At the apartment, Vladimir washes up, and grabs a pillow and blanket from his room while Carrisa takes Tooter out one last time. She tries to protest about taking his bed, but he is having none of that. He is glad that he had just washed his sheets the day before, and they would be somewhat clean for her. Crazy how that is what was going through his mind right before he drifts off into a deep sleep.

Chapter Nine

A loud yapping sound startles Vladimir out of a deep sleep. He cocks one eye open. The sun beams in through the vertical blinds that hang in front of his sliding glass door. He had forgotten that he was sleeping on his couch. *Oh, shit,* Vladimir thinks, *Carrisa is here.*

Vladimir sits up and stretches his limbs before prying open the other eye. Carrisa stands by his bedroom door, a shaking puppy in her arms.

"Good morning," Vladimir croaks out.

"Um, yeah, morning. Not sure if it's a good one for Tooter here. Topsy is pretty tough," Carrisa points her head in the direction of the front door. Topsy is halfway up the door, his tongue lapping out and licking the knob.

"No, Topsy, we aren't going outside right now," Vladimir says passively.

"Um, do you take it outside?" Carrisa asks.

"On the patio sometimes. I have to sit with him, though, because he can slither up and get over the gate.

I've thought about covering it, but I wasn't sure how long I would stay here."

"I don't know where Topsy uses the bathroom, but Tooter needs to go outside. Sorry we woke you, but I didn't want to open the door with him there," Carrisa states.

"Oh, he just goes wherever. That's why I picked this place," Vladimir taps a foot as he stands. "Linoleum floors make it easy to clean."

Vladimir directs topsy over to the dining area, where a dozen aquariums sit all along the walls. One large tank sits on a high stand. In the stand is a rock formation that Topsy slithers into.

"He likes it in there," Vladimir announces. "All clear, you can go out now."

Carissa mumbles, "Thanks," as she heads out the front door. Once she is out there, Vladimir thinks it might not be a good idea to let her go alone, so he rushes out to join them.

He stands off to the side barefoot only wearing his boxers and a Marilyn Manson tee shirt while he watches Carrisa watch Tooter take care of business. He thinks about the young pup and how he must be pretty smart to already be house trained at such a young age and with little consistency in his life.

"Oh, you didn't need to come with," Carrisa says bashfully. When Vladimir first met her, he would have never thought of her as the shy type, but he is learning more every second that they are together.

"Oh, yes, I did. We don't know where Jalal is or what he plans on doing. The police said they would arrest him once the hospital gave the all-clear, but who knows if that stuck, and he didn't get out already."

Carrisa's shoulders sink at Vladimir's admission. "Right, yes, you're right. Come on, Tooter, let's go inside."

Inside, Vladimir checks to make sure Topsy isn't trying to make an escape again before opening the door fully and ushering in his house guests. "You hungry?"

"Yes, oh, that reminds me. The dishes your mom sent you home with last night got trampled during your fight, so I threw them out. I hope that's okay."

"No problem. I wasn't planning on feeding you that for breakfast." Vladimir checks the time; it is only a little past eight in the morning. No wonder he is still tired. Oh well, he is up now. He might as well make the best of it. "You like eggs? I can make us scrambled eggs and toast."

"That sounds great, but you don't have to do that. Hey, listen, I never got a chance to make any calls last night. You think I can use your phone now?" Carrisa asks.

"Help yourself, and I'll be in the kitchen," he says this as if it's a completely separate room and not just right there next to the living room.

Vladimir busies himself with scrambling up half a dozen eggs and toasting four slices of bread. He isn't sure how much she will eat, but he could finish it all off if she is finicky.

Carrisa sits on the couch to make her calls, and he can hear her talking in a hushed yet angry tone to someone on the other end. From what Vladimir can decipher, the call isn't going the way Carrisa had hoped.

Vladimir sets the food on the bar then grabs butter, jelly, and orange juice from the fridge. Once everything is ready, he takes a seat on one of the two stools. He never sits here; his meals are usually enjoyed from the couch while watching mindless television, but he figures she might like to sit up here.

Carrisa ends her last call, disappointment written all over her face. She jumps into the empty stool with a huff then says, "This smells good. Thank you. I can't remember the last time I had something other than cereal or pop tarts for breakfast."

"I'm glad you're here. Otherwise, that's just what I would be having. You gave me a good excuse to use these eggs before they go bad and get tossed over to one of the snakes."

"They eat them?" Carrisa asks.

"Oh yeah, shells and all. Sometimes when I'm feeling generous, I will soft boil them and remove the shells, but they don't care either way." Vladimir swallows a few bites of eggs before he continues. "I still have half a carton; you might just get to see them eat some soon."

"That sounds cool, but I'll get out of your hair today. I know you have work, and you don't need us squatting at your place." Carrisa adds grape jelly to her toast before taking a large bite.

"Nonsense, you saw my family. I am used to always having people around. It's nice having you here."

Vladimir is working his way up to his next question. "How did it go with your mom?"

"Well, I got ahold of her, so that's good." Carrisa doesn't deliver that sentence like it is good news in the least. "She was at work, but she said she couldn't send me the forty-five bucks right now. Oh, by the way, that's how much it would cost to get to Dallas. I checked the schedule, and they have a bus leaving at three today. I also talked to my sister, and she said now isn't a good time, not for giving me money or for me to come stay with her. She has a family, so I understand. It's okay. I will figure it out. You think you can drop me at the station before you go to work?"

"Well, I could, but if you don't have anywhere to go, then I wouldn't want to just leave you there." Vladimir finishes his last bite of eggs then turns to Carrisa. "Look, we should talk about last night, but I really need a shower first. I am going to take a quick one, then I have a lot of questions, if you're willing to answer them."

"I can try," Carrisa responds with a mouthful of eggs and regret in her eyes.

When Vladimir emerges from the shower, he takes a long look at his face. Sure enough, the bruising has started. Not just from the blow his cheek took at work yesterday, but also on his chin. His knuckles are all kinds of fucked up, but he isn't bleeding anywhere, so he doesn't think care is needed. If he had thought about putting an icepack on his face last night, that might have helped, but he figures it isn't worth much now.

He finds Carrisa sitting on the couch, flipping through channels on the television. "You have cable," she says in astonishment.

"Yeah, it's included in the rent. Everyone gets it here."

"Nice," Carrisa says as she settles on Nickelodeon. "Sorry, I like this show, and I haven't seen it in a while."

"All good. Do you want to take a shower? I assume you have some necessities in your massive backpack."

"I do and I will, just not right now. I will before we leave though."

"So, I was a little thrown off that I didn't get arrested last night but glad that you and my neighbor had my back. I never say much to that guy," Vladimir admits, "but he's about to get a fruit basket from me, or something like that.".

"We didn't say anything that wasn't true. I got to talk to him and thanked him for stepping up. He seems nice."

"Anyway, the cops said you made a statement and showed them some marks? What was that about?" Vladimir asks.

There was that look again as if she feels ashamed of just a simple question. The truth is, it isn't so simple. "Look, you've done a lot to help me, and I appreciate it, but I don't think you really want to know all of the details of my fucked-up life. Yes, I made a statement, and the police even tried to talk me into pressing charges against Jalal. However, I just want to put all of that behind me and go home, wherever that may be."

"Did he hurt you?" Vladimir is serious now. If that fucker has laid his hands on her, he has more than a beat-down coming.

"It's not that simple. We've been together since high school. He does love me; he just has a temper. Sometimes he has a hard time relaying his emotions, and he goes the physical route, but he doesn't mean to hurt me. He just doesn't know any better. That's how he was raised. His father and mother fought all the time, and sometimes Jalal got caught up in their mess, and so that's how he deals with stuff."

Is she seriously defending him right now? Vladimir thinks. "You do know that it is never okay for a man to harm a woman, right? Loving someone is no excuse. In fact, if he loves you, then he would never hurt you."

Carrisa lets out a long breath, "You wouldn't understand."

"No, I don't, and I think the majority of the population would agree with me. So, from what the cop said, Jalal did hurt you, and I can only assume you are going to let him get away with it and not press charges?"

"Vlad, that's just a lot of drama, and as I said, I just want to put this all behind me," Carrisa whines and shakes her head as if their conversation is exhausting.

Vladimir places a comforting arm around her shoulder, and to his surprise, she leans into him and accepts his embrace. "I get it, and I am in no way trying to pressure you, but if he hurt you, he needs to pay."

"Well, I did leave him," Carrisa reminds him, looking up at him through her lashes. "He got his ass handed to him last night, went to the hospital, got arrested, and he's losing me. I think that's a lot. At least it's enough for me."

Vladimir shakes his head while staring into her eyes. "If you say so. Still, that fucker would be in the ground if you were my sister."

"Phoebe is a lucky girl to have so many charming brothers," Carrisa says with a smile.

"You think my brothers are charming?" Carrisa just laughs and buries her face into his chest. "She isn't the only one. I have two more that you haven't met yet."

"Wow, your parents were busy," Carrisa states.

"Don't remind me. So, listen," Vladimir says, sitting up a little straighter, causing Carrisa to do the same. "I can give you the forty-five dollars. That's not a problem for me."

"I don't want your money."

"Let me finish," Vladimir chastises. "I'm not going to give it to you. From the sound of it, you don't have much waiting for you in Dallas, and it doesn't sound like anyone that will take you in is going to welcome Tooter. Plus, Jalal can find you there. The police aren't going to keep him long, that is if they even still have him."

"You do know that he can find me here too. I mean, he already did," Carrisa says.

"I know that, but I have another idea. I am not going to tell you yet because I have to talk to someone first, but I think it might work. Just stay here, make yourself at home while I'm working today, and I will see what I can do."

"Why are you being so nice to me?"

"Because I am a nice guy, most of us are. You have just been choosing poorly," Vladimir states, then bites his tongue while waiting for a response.

"Good point." Carrisa pushes off of the couch and out from under Vladimir's arm. She stands then says, "I think I will take that shower now." With that, she leaves Vladimir alone in the living room with only the cast of 'All That' and a sleeping puppy as company.

Chapter Ten

The first chance he gets, Vladimir sits down in the office and calls his mother at the bookstore. He knew that was where he would find her, and he is right. He isn't sure how she would answer the question that he has but given the turmoil the Frazier family had been through in the past, she was always ready to help out someone in need.

"Well, if it isn't my favorite son!" Mary Beth says once Vladimir announces himself.

"I always knew it!" Vladimir replies. "Am I interrupting anything?"

"Not at all. We're dead right now, so I'm just writing. I should thank you. Since you brought that puppy over last night, I got some new inspiration to write about a woman who volunteers at a rescue organization..." Vladimir had to stop her there; he didn't have all the time in the world, and if he let her, she would go on forever.

"That sounds great Mom, can't wait to read it. So, since I am your favorite son, I have a favor to ask. I know you are going to want to grant me this favor since, you know, I brought you inspiration and all."

Mary Beth lets out a sigh, and Vladimir knew she was rolling her eyes at that moment. "That depends on what it is." The enthusiasm from a second ago is long gone.

"Remember Carrisa?"

"I seriously just met her less than twenty-four hours ago. I am not old enough to forget that easily."

"Mom, some shit happened last night, and I don't have time to go over it all right now, but she needs somewhere to go," Vladimir admits.

"Language," Mary Beth chastises before continuing. "How long have you been seeing this girl? You aren't thinking about moving her in with you already, are you?" Mary Beth questions.

"No, and we're not seeing each other; she is just a friend in need, and I want to help. She has no one. Her family is in Dallas, but they are not in a position to help her. I was wondering if you could put her up in the guest room for a little while?"

"How old is she?" Mary Beth asks.

"Nineteen, I think? Or at least, that's what she says."

"You don't even know her enough to know her age. This all sounds really suspicious. You know we can't just be trusting anyone, look what happened last time," Mary Beth reprimands.

"Trust me, it is not like that. Just let me explain everything tonight when I get off work, and you'll understand. She is really sweet, and she just needs some help during a tough time in her life," Vladimir begs.

"You are going to have to talk to your father about this also. I'm not the only one making decisions in my house."

"Sure, Mom, we can include him," Vladimir says with humor in his voice. Everyone knows that Mary Beth would be the one with a final vote on anything in that house. "Can we come over when I get off?"

"You don't have to ask, but I will warn your father about what is to come. I'm not making any promises, though; I am not comfortable with this. It is all a little too soon." Mary Beth pauses for a moment before she continues, "Wait! What about that dog? Is she bringing that dog with her? You know Peter won't be able to handle that."

"Well, I can't keep him at my house unless you want him to end up as snake food."

"Okay, I think we can work something out." With that, they say their goodbyes and end the call.

On his next break, Vladimir calls his apartment. He had told Carrisa she could answer the phone. She was hoping her mom would call her back with better news than she had earlier. Vladimir hopes his news will cheer her up a bit.

"Hello," comes Carrisa's hesitant greeting after the third ring.

"Hey, it's me, Vlad. How is everything?"

"Hi, yeah, everything is okay, quiet."

"So, no visitors or calls?" Vladimir asks.

"No one has come by, but you did get two telemarketing calls. I just hung up on them. I hope that's okay."

"I would have done the same thing," Vladimir laughs.

"So, I see that you have some hamburger meat in the freezer. You know I could make a meatloaf for dinner if you want," Carrisa says.

"That sounds really nice, but I have other plans," Vladimir hears a gush of breath come through the line as if Carrisa is disappointed with his answer. "We are going to go to my parents' house again tonight so we can eat there."

"Are you sure that would be alright? Bringing me two nights in a row? Also, will your mom get mad that I threw out her Tupperware?"

Her constant concern amuses Vladimir. "Trust me, my mom doesn't give me anything she plans on seeing again."

"Okay, but if she asks, I am blaming you."

"Deal. Look, this is a little presumptuous of me, but I asked them if you could stay there for a while. They have a spare room that is already set up for guests, and they are used to more people than what they currently have. They want to talk to you some more, but I figured you might be more comfortable there."

"I told you I could go back to Dallas," Carrisa states.

"And I told you how I felt about that. My parents would agree. If you don't like it there, after a couple of days, hell after one night I promise I will give you the money to take a bus. Okay?" Vladimir waits a few breaths for her response.

Finally, Carrisa says, "Well, I guess it wouldn't hurt anything to go talk to them. They might say no."

"I doubt that Carrisa. After just knowing you for a short time, I would be happy to have you stay with me. I have Topsy and a small apartment, so I know you will be more comfortable over there."

"You might be right. But I wasn't planning on staying and cramping up your life," Carrisa teases, lightening up the dour mood that had seeped into their conversation.

"Okay, have your stuff ready just in case they say yes, and I will scoop you and Tooter up as soon as I get off."

Vladimir gets through his Monday without any unwelcomed visits from Jalal or anyone else. He and Evette close up and get out of there a little after nine. Many people had asked him throughout the day about what had happened to his face, but he just shrugged it off. It wasn't that bad; for all they knew, he slipped while hiking. He thought about using that lie on his parents, but they were going to see right through that one. He was going to be honest and tell them every last detail. This would only help Carrisa. If they thought she was in danger, then the Frazier house was the safest place for her.

Carrisa is visibly nervous when Vladimir parks along the curb and shuts off the engine. She doesn't move when Vladimir turns to her. It is dark inside and outside of the car, but he can make out her features. She almost looks as if she is going to cry.

"Don't stress about it," Vladimir says. "It will either be a yes or no, and if it's a yes, you are going to love it here until my parents over-shower affection onto you, and then you will hate it. And if it's a no, then you'll just come back with me, and we'll figure it out. Okay?"

"Okay," Carrisa replies, not having many other options in her pocket.

Vladimir helps her out of the car then grabs her bag from the back seat. They walk up to the house, and Carrisa tries her best to take it all in. The shutters, the flowers in carefully placed pots, the sign that reads 'Frazier Family Funhouse.' It's a lot, and something deep inside of her wishes they will take her in. She has never had a real family. Sure, she had a mother and an older sister, but things were hard in their house. Her mother struggled to just feed Carrisa and her sister. Sometimes they went without electricity, and there was that one time they were evicted when she was ten, and they had to sleep in their station wagon for a week.

Carrisa felt that if the Fraziers wouldn't accept her, there was no way she could stay at Vladimir's with Tooter, and there was also little chance she could go back to her mother's. Her mom currently lives in a halfway house, for crying out loud. Not because she was a criminal but because she had nowhere else to go, and the state had no other options as far as housing. Her mother worked hard, she didn't do drugs, but she did like her alcohol and cigarettes.

Ms. Abbott works fifty hours a week as a clerk at a convenience store and still can't afford rent on the cheapest of apartments. Once Carrisa turned eighteen, she knew she had to leave. Her mother had done the best job she could have done, and Carrisa knew her limits. Her sister had done the same thing she had. Once Alice turned eighteen, she shacked up with James and started popping out babies. The only difference is that James wasn't an obsessive, abusive asshole.

Carrisa knew she had fucked up the first time Jalal laid his hands on her. She had seen it coming; it was a slow build that was impossible to sidestep. He was an angry man from the beginning, but he got her out of her poverty-stricken childhood, put a roof over her head, gave her food and clothes. For that, she was grateful, and thought a few bruises and tear-filled nights were worth it. She wasn't going to be like her sister though. Alice may act like she is happy, but she settled, and Carrisa was not going to be stuck with that asshole because of a child; she always made him pull out. God forbid she got pregnant; that jerk would have probably beat the baby out of her.

Looking at the house with different eyes than she did on her first visit, she really hopes Mary Beth and Michael say yes.

Vladimir opens the door and motions for Carrisa to enter, the smell of something amazing hitting her senses immediately. "Let's eat first. My parents usually eat earlier, but they waited on us."

"Oh, well, now I feel bad," Carrisa says.

"Don't, that was their choice, they wanted to wait. Fairly sure my brothers didn't, though," Vladimir admits.

"Your brothers still live here?" Carrisa asks a look of shock on her face. She doesn't know why but for some reason, she thought it was just Mary Beth and Michael in this big house.

"Yeah, two of them, the same ones you met yesterday."

They enter the kitchen just as Mary Beth is pulling a casserole out of the oven. "Oh, goody, you're here."

"Do you need help with anything?" Carrisa is eager to lend a hand wherever it is needed.

Mary Beth sets the dish down and gives Carrisa an approving look. "Usually, yes. But not tonight. Everything is all set. You two wash up. Peter and Elan should be here any second, and then we can dig in. Michael, please put Tooter out back while we eat." Michael does as his wife instructs.

Just then, the front door slams shut, and Michael yells at the boys about slamming his doors. The people in the kitchen can hear mumbles coming from Peter and Elan but can't make out what they are saying.

"Boys, hurry up. We are sitting down now," Mary Beth calls to her children.

They make their way to the dining room and take their seats as Elan and Peter wash up in the kitchen. Once the two join the rest of the family and see Vladimir and Carrisa, they stop in their tracks.

"Well, hello again," Elan says. "Did you love my mother's cooking so much that you had to come back for more, or is Vlad here holding you hostage?"

"A little of both," Carrisa teases. When no one joins in on her jokes, she rushes to say, "No, he is not holding me hostage. I should clarify that I am here of my own free will."

"Okay, just checking," Elan adds as he scoops almost half of the casserole onto his plate before sitting down. Carrisa sees that the paranoia thing runs in the family. Mary Beth slaps Elan's hand, and he releases half of it back into the dish.

Mary Beth clears her throat, "You will have to excuse my children, Carrisa. These three here," she motions to Michael, Peter, and Elan, "are used to getting the leftover casserole all to themselves. They have forgotten their manners tonight," Mary Beth chastises.

"Leftover casserole?" Carrisa questions.

"Yes, see, I cook every night, and sometimes the fridge gets overloaded with leftovers. Take all the meats, potatoes, starches, and veggies, you throw those in a pan, then add cheese, and you have yourself a mighty fine casserole dish."

"Sounds delicious. We didn't have leftovers in my house. If you didn't get it while the getting was good, you were shit out of luck." Carrisa notices Mary Beth's raised brow and adds, "Sorry, please excuse my language."

"Mom, you better get the soap," Elan pipes in.

"Oh, please, boy, it was a minor slip. I am sure it will not happen again," Mary Beth says. "I hope you enjoy it; we all usually do."

"I am sure that I will, ma'am," Carrisa says bashfully before digging into her food.

Once everyone is done, the boys stand to clear the table but Mary Beth motions for them to stop and have a seat.

"I really think we should all be here for this, if that is okay with you two," Mary Beth looks to Vladimir and Carrisa for approval.

"Yeah, I mean, I guess so," Carrisa responds when she sees that Vladimir has not intervened.

"Okay then," Michael starts. "So, what is going on here?"

"Carrisa needs a place to stay for a bit. She is from Dallas, but I don't believe that her family in Dallas is the best place for her right now," Vladimir answers.

"I would like to hear from her, but first, what the hell happened to your face?" Michael asks his son.

"Well," Vladimir starts, "that has a lot to do with why Carrisa needs somewhere to go. She has this boyfriend…"

"Ex-boyfriend," Carrisa pipes in.

"Sorry, ex-boyfriend. He kicked her out, then when she came to me for help, he came after me with a baseball bat." Everyone gasps at that. "Don't worry, he didn't get far with that bat. I actually beat the shit out of him."

"Language," Mary Beth interrupts.

"Sorry. Anyway, he met us outside of my apartment last night after we left here, and he was ready to do some damage. However, he got arrested because Carrisa and my neighbor gave a statement that they saw the entire thing and I was acting in self-defense. I don't know if anything will come of last night's incident, but I feel for

Carrisa's safety, and since the guy knows where I live, I don't think it's safe for her to stay there while I'm at work."

Carrisa's heart skips a beat. She had not thought about it that way. She had assumed that Vladimir was just putting her off onto someone else, but now it makes sense. He feared that Jalal would come back while Carrisa was alone and try to harm her when she didn't have Vladimir to protect her.

Vladimir goes on, "There is always someone here at the house, and I thought her and Tooter would be safe with you guys around. Also, that fool doesn't know where you live, and he isn't a Tyler native, so he wouldn't know where to look."

"Wait, the dog. Is the dog staying here too?" Peter asks.

"Chill out, son, we can manage a small puppy like him. She can keep him in her room and outside; you don't have to worry about having a freaking asthma attack," Michael says.

"So, is that a yes?" Carrisa asks.

"Not so fast," Mary Beth adds. "We have some questions of our own." She can tell by her son's words that he cares for this girl, but she still needs to take some precautions.

Carrisa places her palms on the table and starts, "My name is Carrisa Abbot. I am nineteen. I graduated high school last year and moved here with my ex-boyfriend Jalal at the beginning of this past summer. We started dating at the end of junior year, and after graduation, he

LEIGH M. HALL

got a job here in Tyler, so I moved with him. There wasn't ever any question as to if I would join him or not. My home life was never great, and my mom basically said I had to go after graduation. I did love him, but stuff had already gotten physical at that point. The thing is, I never felt like I had any other options." Carissa takes a long breath. She is trying to get this all out in one go.

"I didn't have the greatest GPA, so no scholarships were offered to me, and there was no way I could afford to even go to community college, much less live and eat while attending it. The only option I had for survival was to follow Jalal. Don't judge me, please. As I said, I did love him, and he did provide for me as promised, but then one day, I found Tooter, and Jalal just became this horrible being. It didn't happen overnight but the way he acted towards Tooter was an eye-opener. I couldn't stand him anymore, and I think he could sense that."

Carrisa takes a break and looks around the table. Everyone has their full attention on what she has to say next. "I didn't mean for all of that to happen to Vlad last night. He was only trying to help, and I have not had anyone help me in a long time, so I will be eternally grateful to him. Your family is incredible. I have never seen anything like it besides on TV, and even then, it's not the same because you guys are so real. I would really like to stay here for a little while, just until I can get on my own feet, not again, but for the first time. I have never been given that chance, and Vlad here says that you might be able to help me with that."

"Thank you for sharing your story with us." Mary Beth folds her hands into her lap then looks over at Elan. "Elan, go get Tooter, will you? He has been scratching at that back door for the past five minutes. Peter, Vlad, you can start clearing the table."

Carrisa just sits there as the table is cleared around her. She hears Elan get her puppy, but the puppy is not brought to her. She isn't sure what is happening right now, but the anticipation is killing her. Are these people going to let her stay or are they going to throw her out on her ass just like everyone else in her life has?

Once the boys are gone, Mary Beth speaks again, "You have some personal belongings?"

"Some, Vladimir set them in the front room."

Mary Beth stands from the table and says, "Collect your bags, and I will show you to your room."

Carrisa is elated. She cannot believe her luck. They are actually going to let her stay in this amazing house, with this spectacular family. So many things are running through Carrisa's mind just then, but on top of it all is her appreciation for what Vladimir has done for her.

Chapter Eleven

That next day, Vladimir had tried calling the house to talk to Carrisa, but his father stated that she was across the street with his mother working on Bethany's garden for Nigel.

On Wednesday, Vladimir tried again, but apparently, Carrisa was out with Mary Beth, and Michael had no idea when they would be back.

Vladimir was starting to get worried until he finally received a call late Thursday night.

"Hello?" Vladimir answers the line.

"Hey, Vlad, how's it hanging?" Carrisa asks from the other end.

"Low and a little to the left." Vladimir immediately slaps himself on the forehead. "Sorry, that's my auto-response for my friends. You shouldn't have heard that. Please wipe it from your memory."

"What are you talking about? I didn't hear anything," Carrisa chuckles.

"Good," Vladimir lets out a breath in relief. "How are things over there? I have been trying to reach you, but apparently, you have been busy."

"You can say that again," Carrisa agrees. "Your mom is so much fun! You didn't tell me how much fun I would be having. We are constantly doing shit, like all the time. And I got a job! Can you believe that?"

"You got a job? That's great. Where?"

"Well, first off, you didn't tell me that your mother is a writer either. I was kind of taken off guard when she asked me if I liked to read. Like, read what? No one has ever asked me that before. I was like, read what, an instruction manual on how to put together a coffee table? Because to me, reading was a chore in school. I read what was dished out, and that was it. I had no idea you guys owned a bookstore. So, yeah, I now have a job at said bookstore. I just started today, so it is all kind of new to me. But I liked it. Vlad, I have never in my life had a job before. This feels amazing."

"I am guessing that the job is a good thing," Vladimir says this as a statement and not a question.

"She said that your sister Tallulah worked there and that they haven't hired anyone since she went off to college. You never said you have a sister named Tallulah. First Phoebe and now Tallulah; what cool names. Anyway, yeah, so it is badass. I am going to work this week with your mom, then maybe next week I can be on my own. I am so stoked." She sounds more like the Carrisa that Vladimir had met that first time in the pet store and less like the abused one he had seen last.

"Tallulah is the youngest, and yeah, she loves to read. She is actually an English major and planning on becoming a writer."

"Your mom said that she is coming home for Thanksgiving in a couple of weeks, and I can't wait to meet her. She sounds amazing. So, another thing that's going on with me is that I never got a driver's license. Your mom is going to take me next week to see about taking the test; I just need to get the proper ID in order first. She has been letting me drive around for the last couple of days, and to be honest, I have been driving for years. My mother started letting me drive at ten when she was too drunk to do it herself. So, I am a natural. Your mom is amazing. Did I already say that? Your dad is pretty quiet, but he is cool; he said that y'all also own a gun shop, and he will take me and teach me how to shoot this weekend. Bad fucking ass! I am excited about that, but I also am kind of worried when your sisters and your other brother Penn come into town. Like I haven't met them before and also, do they need the room I am staying in? By the way, I really love the room."

Vladimir tries to gather his thoughts before he speaks; she had just spat a lot out to him at once. "Well, I'm pretty sure Tallulah's room is just how she left it. My mom might make a bed for Penn in my old room or wherever, and Poppy and her girlfriend will get a hotel just as they always do, so I don't think you need to worry about where you will sleep. I'm glad that you like it; I knew that you would, but I was a little worried."

"No need to worry. I love it here, and I do know that it is temporary, but at the same time, I am embracing it all," Carrisa admits. "You haven't heard from him, have you?"

They both knew who she was talking about, no need to mention a name. "No, nothing, let's hope it stays that way."

Carrisa waits a moment before she responds, "I hope so, but that isn't like him. He always has to have the last word. I feel like we haven't seen the last of him."

"Just so you know," Vladimir starts, "if he does try anything now, he will be in some deep shit. My family doesn't play those games. That mother fucker will regret ever looking in your direction."

"Oh, I get that," Carrisa replies. "I would never want to be on bad terms with your folks. Let's hope you taught him a lesson with that beat down." Carrisa hesitates before saying her next line, "So, Elan has been super helpful with Tooter, and everyone loves him. Phoebe brought Hannah over yesterday so they could play, and Hannah asked if she could keep him. I didn't say yes, but Phoebe said they would take him to her house if I was okay with it. Peter is having a hard time. He can't take antihistamines during the day because they make him sleepy, and I don't like keeping Tooter outside. So, I said yes. I hope you're not mad. This way, we still get to see him, and he has kids to play with. Hannah fucking loves him."

"The amount of swear words you still use after being around my mother for so long boggles my mind," Vladimir admits.

"Oh, I am just trying to get them all out now, so I don't have any left to use in her presence," Carrisa laughs.

"Fair enough. That's good about Tooter, and it was about time Hannah got a pet. Say, listen. Some friends and I get together on Friday nights at a local place, and I was wondering if you would like to join us?" Vladimir asks.

"Actually, I will be there because Elan already invited me. He and Addy said they went there last week, and you weren't there, and I realized that it was because of me. You weren't doing your regular Friday night thing because you were taking care of my dog. I feel so bad about that, and so, yes, I will be there, and I am excited to hang out with you again," Carrisa admits.

"Okay then, I guess I will see you on Friday." With that, they end their call, and Vladimir is left floating on a cloud of hope.

Friday took forever to come. Vladimir could have bet that his past week was actually an entire year in disguise. He had never witnessed days so long or nights so lonely. He longed for his boring day off, where he could clean house and hike the woods and not give a fuck about anything else. Thankfully, now Friday is here, and he gets to see Carrisa tonight.

Vladimir arrives at The Railroad before any of his friends do. Hell, he arrives there before half the staff does. He is so eager to see Carrisa again that he just changed after work and headed straight there. The place doesn't even get hot until ten, but Vladimir doesn't care. He sits there and nurses a single beer until Philip arrives first.

"Hey, man," Philip says as he approaches Vladimir at his table. "You snagged a good spot."

"That happens when you're here before anyone else," Vladimir replies.

"That so? Anyway, man, Arleen and her, whatever he is, are coming tonight, so I am going to grab a pitcher and take up one of these seats for the show. You know how she gets with her flings. This should be entertaining," Philip says as he chuckles and heads off to the bar.

As soon as Philip leaves, Elan, Addy, Peter, and Carrisa enter the bar. Vladimir does not like the way this looks; Peter seems way too comfortable with Carrisa walking beside him. While Elan comes up to greet him, Vladimir moves past him and takes Carrisa in for a long, needed hug. "Hey," Vladimir says, "I am so glad you made it. It feels like forever since I last saw you."

"I know, right," Carrisa responds in a cheerful tone. "It has only been a few days, but so much has happened."

"Come, I saved us a large booth. Can I get you something to drink?" Vladimir asks.

Carrisa takes a seat and says, "I will have a Dr. Pepper."

"Are you sure," Vladimir asks. "This place doesn't care, and you can have alcohol if you want."

"I never touch the stuff. My mother is a recovering alcoholic. I watched what it did to her, and I have no desire to go down that same road," Carrisa states with a nod of finality.

"One Dr. Pepper coming up," Vladimir says before rushing off to the bar.

Vladimir goes to the bar with every intention of getting himself another beer, but he knows everyone around Carrisa will be drinking tonight, and he doesn't want her to feel left out. He had only had one beer, one he had sipped on for almost an hour. That one beer gave him no satisfaction, so he decides to get two Dr. Peppers and join her in a sugar rush instead.

When Vladimir returns to the table, it is full, and Carrisa's attention is caught up in the conversation she is having with Addy.

"Oh, you have to, it is a tradition in these parts. Even if you don't know how to sing, everyone around here will be too drunk to notice," Addy proclaims.

"I don't know," Carrisa says as she buries her head into her chest and her cheeks heat up with embarrassment.

"What is she trying to make you do?" Vladimir asks when he sets their drinks down and looks Addy in the eyes. She just smiles at him and points to Carrisa.

"She is trying to get me on stage to sing, and that is not going to happen," Carrisa says into her chest.

"Oh, well, we will see about that," Vladimir laughs.

"Not you too," Carrisa whines while looking up at him, then sees her drink and grabs it for a sip.

"I am just saying that it is fun, and you are living at the Frazier house now. Karaoke is sort of our thing," Vladimir admits.

"You sing?" Carrisa looks at him with a curious expression. Vladimir does not look like someone you would see on a karaoke stage. With his dyed jet-black hair, pale skin, and brow piercing. He looks more like someone you would see in a mosh pit.

"I can, you might not want to hear it, but it is not impossible."

"Well, this I have to see!" Carrisa exclaims.

"Oh, Vlad doesn't do that shit here, not with people watching," Peter pipes in with a mischievous smile. Vladimir does not like where Peter is going with this, as if he is daring him to step on that stage and prove him wrong. Vladimir does not care what others think, and no matter how much banter they throw his way, he isn't doing it.

The night moves on much faster than the week had for Vladimir. The Railroad is packed just as it is every Friday night. By midnight everyone that is drinking is pretty lit, and Peter has even managed to set his attention on someone besides Carrisa. Vladimir is glad that Peter has started to move on after that shit he and Tallulah tried to pull a couple of years ago. Peter hasn't had anyone steady, but he has sampled a few girls here and there. Vladimir needed him to do more than sample to get that horrible picture of his siblings out of his head, but it is slowly fading away.

Addy does manage to get Carrisa on stage to sing 'I'm Only Happy When It Rains' with her, and they do alright. Vladimir likes Addy; she is just what Elan needs in his life. He also learns that she has a five-year-old son, and Elan got the privilege of meeting him recently. Watching his brother talk about that little boy makes Vladimir want a connection like that in his life. *Hold up, where did that come from? Slow the fuck down*, Vladimir thinks to himself.

The crowd starts to clear out around one in the morning. Elan, Peter, and Carrisa had all ridden together in Addy's car. They close their tabs and head for the exit as a group. Vladimir walks Carrisa to the rear passenger door, not wanting the night to end but also not knowing how to say goodbye. He knows he will see her again on Sunday but giving her more than a hug is not something he wants to do in front of his brothers.

Everyone is already in the car; all the windows are rolled down, and Vladimir can hear them bickering about what song to play for the ride home. It is only a ten-minute drive to the house, so this is a crucial choice. Vladimir finally gives Carrisa a small hug, tells her he had fun, and waits for her to sit in her seat before closing the door and walking off. He is high as a kite, and he wants more—wants it bad.

Chapter Twelve

Just as Vladimir starts to walk toward his car, he hears someone call out to him from a corner of the parking lot that is hidden in the shadows of a large tree.

"I see you are making yourself mighty comfortable with my girl!" Vladimir can't see him, but he doesn't need to; he knows who it is, and just like last time, the fucking creep is hiding.

"I see you got out," Vladimir replies, stopping in the middle of the parking lot. Addy hasn't pulled out yet, and he can still hear them switching between stations in her Chevy Cavalier.

"Yeah, your little bitch-ass didn't press charges, so they let me go," Jalal says as he starts to move closer, and Vladimir can now see a little of his face.

"Damn!" Vladimir gasps when he gets a good look at him. The dude is fucked! Half of his face is swollen to twice its size. He has lacerations on his forehead, and there are some gnarly stitches running across his bottom lip. "Thought maybe you suffered enough. I mean, look at you. Your face looks like it went through a shredder. You lost your girl, and you are left being you. No one would want that. I thought maybe I'd would give you a break."

Red lights shimmer across the concrete as Addy slowly backs up and moves to exit the parking lot. Right as there is a lull in the song that plays inside the car, Jalal decides to get loud.

"Big fucking mistake, asshole!" Then Jalal comes gunning for him. As Vladimir watches the idiot head his way, he wonders why he keeps doing this. The last two times Jalal tried tackling him down, it got him nowhere but the floor, the hospital, and then jail.

Apparently, the people in the car heard Jalal yelling. Elan motioned for Addy to stop because just as Jalal is about to reach Vladimir, just as he pulls out the blade that was hidden up his sleeve, Addy's car comes to a skidding halt. All four doors open as soon as the blade meets Vladimir's abdomen. He had every intention of sidestepping and pushing Jalal off, but seeing the blade then hearing the car stop messes with his focus, and he underestimated Jalal's speed.

Jalal doesn't stop there; he quickly pulls out the knife then shoves it back in, this time a little higher, this time hitting Vladimir in a rib, causing the tip of the blade to break off into the bone. He doesn't get to do any more damage, though; Peter and Elan are on him in an instant. Carrisa and Addy stand by the car and start to scream when they see all the blood coming from Vladimir's chest. His white button-up shirt is slowly turning red.

Before Vladimir can comprehend what had just happened, before his knees can hit the paved ground, Carrisa is at his side. She grabs ahold of one arm, trying to keep him from landing on his face. She sees that the blade is still inside him, and she holds his body up so that he does not fall forward and cause more damage than what has already been done.

By this time, people from inside The Railroad have already started to filter out to see what the commotion is all about. Addy yells for them to call 911, and Vladimir can barely hear her. The pounding of his own blood coursing through his veins is so loud that it is deafening in his ears. He feels at his stomach then holds his hand out in front of his face. While looking at all the blood, he notices his brother going to town on Jalal as he peeks between his fingers.

Jalal is on the ground, his feet kicking furiously but getting him nowhere. Peter kicks him in the side with his boot as Elan straddles his chest and plows into Jalal's face with both fists. *Oh, God, what is happening?* Vladimir thinks. Of all the ways he thought this night could end, this was not anywhere within the realm of possibilities.

Jalal's legs are no longer kicking. Vladimir can't trust his vision at this point; it is blurry, and he is having a hard time keeping his eyes open. One of the waitresses leans down in front of him with a towel and presses it to the wound that the knife isn't sticking out of. He can faintly hear her and Carissa talking about what they should do. They both agree to leave the knife where it is until the paramedics can get here.

"Sweetie, just breathe slowly. Help will be here soon," the woman says. *Does she even know what she is doing?* Vladimir thinks.

As if she can hear his thoughts, or maybe he said it aloud, he doesn't know, she says, "Don't worry, I am a nursing student. I know what I am doing."

By the time EMS and the police arrive, Jalal is unconscious, and Vladimir is pretty close to joining him. They assess Vladimir first, but when one of the paramedics sees Jalal, Elan freaks out.

"Leave that mother fucker there to die!" Elan yells. The man freezes, not wanting to leave the apparently injured man unattended but also a little scared of Elan. "Take care of Vlad. That is why you were called. Fuck that asshole. If my brother dies on your watch, then you are fucking next."

The two emergency workers are torn on what to do but decide to call for backup and load Vladimir into the ambulance. Vladimir is starting to waver in and out from the loss of blood. Carrisa hops into the ambulance, but the guy sitting in the back with him holds up a hand.

"Are you family?" He asks.

Elan pokes his head into the still open doors, and with an air of confidence and authority states, "She is. She can ride with him." He turns toward Carrisa, "We're right behind you, don't leave his side. I'm going to go inside and call Mom and Dad before we head to the hospital.

Mom will kill me if I don't call her right now." Carrisa just nods in agreement. The doors are shut, the driver gets in his seat, and they are off.

At the hospital, Vladimir is rushed into emergency surgery. Carrisa is ushered to the waiting area and given instructions that she tries her best to remember. The Fraziers will be here soon, and they will want to know what's going on. Right now, she is covered in Vladimir's blood and has no idea how things got this far out of hand.

She never thought Jalal was capable of this. Sure he hit her sometimes, but he never harmed anyone else that she knew of. Why would he do this? He was the one that kicked her out for crying out loud! She didn't have to wait long to try and remember what the doctor had told her. Just a few minutes later, a frantic Mary Beth comes running in through the double doors. The look on her face almost kills Carrisa right there and then.

"What's happening?" Mary Beth asks as she grips tightly to Carrisa's shoulders.

Carrisa struggles with her response, "Uh, um, okay. They said that they were taking him in for x-rays first. The knife was still in him, so they couldn't do an MRI yet. He has lost a lot of blood, but he was conscious, so that is a good sign. After the x-rays, they are going to go into surgery, depending on the results. The doctor said he would be back over for an update before surgery, though."

"Oh, God, I cannot believe this is happening again. Why the hell is this happening?" MaryBeth falls into her husband's chest. Michael is trying his best to stay strong, to hold it together for his wife, but everyone can tell that he is hanging on by a thread.

"Let's just see what they have to say before we lose our minds, shall we?" Michael advises.

Carrisa, Michael, Peter, Mary Beth, and Nigel all sit in the waiting room and do just that; they wait. Addy and Elan were stuck talking to the police after a second ambulance came by to collect Jalal. The police would want to talk to Vladimir, Carrisa, and Peter eventually, but they know that his life is on the line right now and aren't going to push it. They also know what the Frazier family had been through in the past and that this might not be the best time; better to wait and see if Vladimir recovers from his wounds.

After forty-five minutes, the doctor finally comes back with more news. "Hi," he says, approaching the group. "Are you Vladimir's parents?" He asks the only two people among them that could be. When they nod a response, he continues, "He has suffered a great amount of blood loss but nothing fatal at this point. We have been able to successfully stop the blood loss and suture the open wound. No vital organs were disturbed. He is stable right now, coherent, and understands everything we have told him thus far. At this time, we are going to move forward with surgery for the second wound to remove a metal fragment that was left in one of his ribs. He is being prepped as we speak. We are going to attempt to remove the blade and the fragment, during which he will be under sedation.

"His blood type is A positive, and we have some on stand-by in case he needs it during surgery. This surgery could take several hours, and we will keep you updated as it progresses. Rest assured that he is in good hands, and there is a high probability of a full recovery, given time. If you plan on staying, I recommend that you get some coffee from the cafeteria. It is open twenty-four hours. Make yourselves comfortable; you may be here for a while."

"Thank you so much, please take care of my baby," Mary Beth cries out while gripping the doctor's hand tightly. "Sorry," she says while releasing his hand, "You are going to need that soon."

"That I am," the doctor states with a smile. "I will be back upon completion of the surgery. Please wash up, get some rest, or get something to eat while you wait." With that, he makes his exit and leaves the family to worry on their own.

Chapter Thirteen

Vladimir wakes with a start. Machines beep around him, his limbs feel numb and restricted, and his mouth is dry. The first thing that comes into focus is Carrisa's beautiful face.

"You're awake," she says as she hovers above him. "Your mom was just here, but she went to get more coffee. Everyone is here. We are all waiting to see how you feel."

Vladimir tries to sit up but fails. "Um, uh," he coughs out.

Carrisa places a warm palm on his chest, and it is the best feeling he has felt in a long time. *How long have I been out?* Vladimir thinks.

"Don't speak and don't move. Let me get the nurse. I'm not sure what you are allowed to do, and they told us to get them if you wake up."

Carrisa rushes hesitantly from the room. She doesn't fully exit, just holds the door open with her body and hollers out to whoever will listen that he is awake and in need of attention. A set of nurses come in and assess his vitals, then assure him that everything looks okay and that the doctor will be in soon.

Vladimir is dizzy with all the ins and outs, all the instructions and demands that are thrown his way. Before he knows it, his mother is leaning over him with tears in her eyes. Carrisa stands back in the corner as she tries to stay out of Mrs. Frazier's way.

"Mom, I am okay," Vladimir finally says, breaking up his mother's breakdown.

"I know, and I am so grateful. You have no idea how grateful I am for you and this girl right here." She motions in Carrisa's direction, but Carrisa just stands up straight and looks wide-eyed at Vladimir as if she has no idea what Mary Beth could be grateful for. If anything, Carrisa was the cause of all of this. None of this would have happened if Carrisa wasn't in the picture.

Vladimir tries to sit up and comfort his mother, but she stops him. "No, you rest. You need your rest. I am going to take Carrisa home. She needs a shower and a good night's sleep even though it's now four in the morning. You just rest, and I will be back soon." Vladimir gives her a nod, knowing that it will do no good to argue with her. Carrisa comes by to squeeze his hand before she leaves, and he offers her a sad smile.

Vladimir spends the next week in the hospital, recovering from his wounds. The police had stopped by on the third day and taken his statement. Because of the history between Vladimir and Jalal, they knew it was self-defense, but he was worried about his brothers getting into trouble for beating the guy so badly. Apparently, he had suffered several facial fractures, a clavicle fracture, and multiple blows to the ribs and left kidney had done some damage. However, Vladimir didn't need to press charges this time. The police were charging him with attempted murder since he showed up with a blade and followed through in using it.

Once Vladimir is released, he goes home to discover that Mary Beth, Michael, and Elan had been taking turns with the care of his pets. Topsy and everyone else lived as if nothing had happened. He feels a little disdain from that as if his presence and care for his creatures every day were obsolete, but he's still glad that the family thought about his beloved reptiles.

Mary Beth refuses to let Vladimir go home on his own and sends the last person he thought would want to help, Peter. Peter hates the snakes but loves his brother more. He is willing to sleep on the couch even though the notorious Topsy is lurking underneath. Work had granted Vladimir a sabbatical. They felt bad about not stepping in sooner. After the incident that happened at Pet Palace, they could have done something to stop all of this, but Vladimir assured them that it was far beyond their control.

Thanksgiving is a couple of days away, and Vladimir is looking forward to seeing Carrisa again but not looking forward to much else. He doesn't want to face his family after what had happened. He also does not want to face the police and deal with the impending trial that is to come. He knows that there will be one. Jalal is going to face a sentence on his attempted homicide charge, and he wants nothing to do with it. Unfortunately, he is the one Jalal attempted to murder, so he will have to be there.

He has to deal with this one day at a time; it is the only way to get through it. He has no control over anything but his own actions, and he will act accordingly.

Chapter Fourteen

On Thanksgiving Eve, Vladimir received some good news. Jalal pled guilty; he knew that if he tried to fight it, other charges would come to light, so smart move on his part. Vladimir had gotten the call and waited till Thanksgiving dinner to relay the news to everyone else.

He knew his entire family would be there, including Carrisa, who had recently become an honorary member. Carrisa had tried to pull back. She thought that this had all been her fault, and that may be partially true, but Mary Beth reminded her that we could not control other people's actions. That this happened because of Jalal, his decisions, and his actions, and it had nothing to do with her. If it wasn't Vladimir, then it would have been someone else eventually.

It took Carrisa a while to accept that, but she finally did and was able to move forward. Once she was able to get past that minor setback, she set forth with the plans that Mary Beth and Michael had for her. She was scheduled to get her driver's license the first week of December and had all the documents she needed. She loved working at the bookstore and loved staying at the Frazier house even more.

Peter drives Vladimir over to their parents' house for Thanksgiving dinner. Vladimir still isn't up to driving just yet. When they enter the house, they are greeted with an overwhelming amount of love. Tallulah brought home her new boyfriend, Sawyer. Poppy is there with her girlfriend, Ingrid. Elan invited Addy and her son Chad; they can't stay long as they have to get to her parents by five. Penn shows up solo, not too happy to find Elan getting comfortable with his high school crush, but Vladimir can't delve into their problems at the moment. Phoebe is dealing with a fussy baby while Mark chases a rambunctious Hannah around the living room. Yes, everything seems normal in Vladimir's eyes, or as normal as things could ever be in the Frazier home.

He is glad to deal with some normal for once. Vladimir had missed this, the chaotic state of his large family. He had spent way too much time alone, and right now, he is glad to be in the middle of this beautiful mess.

They have dinner, everyone pitching in where they could once all the excitement had died down and the table was clean. Vladimir asks Carrisa to join him on the back patio—alone. She doesn't know what to expect, but she has been wanting to talk to him.

Once they are settled on the patio, Vladimir starts at the same time Carrisa does. "I wanted to…" they both say.

"You go first," Vladimir prompts.

"Okay," Carrisa says bashfully as she looks at her fists in her lap. "I just wanted to say that I am sorry for all of… well, all of this. You wouldn't be in this predicament if it wasn't for me, and I feel like shit because of it. I know you and your family keep saying that it wasn't my fault, but I can't help but feel the opposite. I feel like I should just go."

"They are right, you know," Vladimir states. "You have no control over other people's actions, and as my mother said, if it wasn't me, then it would have been someone else. Jalal was a loose cannon just waiting to explode. He needed to be put in his place, and that place is prison. Now he will be. He pleaded guilty, and he will serve his time, whatever time the judge decides to give him. I know you love a part of him, but also know that he might get the rehabilitation that he needs to be a better person. You helped make that happen. It could have been worse. You could have never met me, and his charges could have been a lot more than attempted homicide and for actual homicide, and you would not be sitting here with me now."

"So true," Carrisa agrees. "How did you get so smart?"

"Well, I was raised in this house," Vladimir gestures to the house around them. He then leans in and does something he has been longing to do for a while. Something he has wanted to do since the moment he met Carrisa that Friday night at Pet Palace. He kisses her. Not just a light, friendly kiss but a wholehearted 'I want you' kind of kiss. One that brings her to her knees and makes her weak. But Vladimir catches her, and he will be there to catch her every time from here on out. Anytime she stumbles or slips, anytime she thinks she might be about to fall, he will catch her. He makes a silent vow to himself, and this is enough. He knows he will not break it, for Carrisa is the first person to plow through his barrier.

Looking into her eyes, he knows that he will do anything for her. He knows that she is the one and nothing will break them apart, not ever.

Chapter Fifteen

Eight months later...

Today is Stephan's first birthday party. It is a big deal; the entire family is coming in for the event. Mary Beth has been working diligently on every last detail. The party is happening in the Frazier's backyard. They have a bounce house, a face painter, and even a snow cone machine.

Phoebe and Mark have been struggling this past year; two small children at such an immature age will do that to you. Mary Beth is doing everything in her power to remind her daughter about the joys of parenting. So, she took on every task herself.

Carrisa has officially become one of the family. She practically runs the bookstore on her own. Several improvements have happened under her watch and Mary Beth is eternally grateful for her presence. She still lives with the Frazier's but spends a lot of time over at Vladimir's apartment.

Today, Vladimir has a surprise for her. Since the entire family will be present at the party, he figures now would be the best time to do this. The only person that is in on his secret is Hannah. She is turning out to be a bright young girl. He needs her help, and with a pinky-promise, he knows his secret is safe with his niece.

Once everyone has arrived, and the party gets started, Vladimir calls upon Hannah to do her thing. She is eager to get this right. Vladimir helps her with her task then asks her to wait with Tooter by the back door till he gives her the signal.

Mary Beth had already called everyone's attention so they could sing happy birthday then have cake. Vladimir steps in once everyone has gathered and interrupts.

"Before we sing to little man here, I have something I need to ask one of you." They all look around, wondering who he is talking about. Vladimir lets out a loud whistle then gets down on one knee in front of Carrisa, who he has pulled front and center, before the crowd.

As soon as his knee hits the grass, Tooter comes rushing his way. He picks up the now forty-pound dog and holds him out to Carrisa.

"What's this?" Carrisa asks in a confused tone. Mary Beth lets out a little sob, instinctively knowing where this is going.

"Tooter has something to ask you," Vladimir states with a hopeful smile on his face.

"Oh, yeah. What's that, Toots?"

Vladimir gives the dog a little shake so that his name tags chime together. "Take a look, I think he wrote it down for you."

Carrisa leans forward and takes the tags between two fingers. He has one that has his info on it but there is a new one. One that says, '*Will you please marry Vladimir, pretty please?*' Carrisa drops the tags and immediately covers her mouth with the same hand that held the tags.

"Well, what do you say?" Vladimir asks as he sets the dog down and reaches for the hand that isn't on her lips. "Will you do me the honor of being my wife?"

Everyone around gasps in unison. Vladimir can faintly hear his sister Tallulah cheering something.

"Are you going to answer him?" Penn asks.

"YES! Oh, my, God, YES!" Carrisa shouts.

Vladimir stands and takes Carrisa in his arms. His entire family is now cheering for them both. Well, everyone besides Stephan who has no idea what is going on and wonders why he hasn't been given any cake yet.

That night, Vladimir takes Carrisa back to his apartment —their apartment. She packs a small bag, but Vladimir tells her they will be back soon for the rest of her stuff. That from now on, his home is her home, wherever that may be.

The ring that he had slipped on her finger earlier that day is small but perfect. One carat, princess cut, a solitaire diamond resting upon a dainty gold band.

Carrisa cannot stop staring at it as she lays in bed, waiting for Vladimir to finish brushing his teeth.

"I can't believe you managed to keep this from me," Carrisa calls out. "You are really bad at keeping secrets, you know."

"I am not!" Vladimir hollers back with a mouth full of toothpaste.

"Okay, I take it back. You are really bad about keeping secrets from me, not other people," Carrisa corrects.

Vladimir exits the bathroom and leans against the wall, wearing nothing but a towel wrapped around his waist. "That may be true, but I was hell-bent on making this a surprise. I hope Stephan isn't too upset that I stole his birthday thunder."

"He might need some therapy, but he will get over it eventually." Carrisa laughs and looks back at her ring.

"Do you like it?" Vladimir asks as he makes his way to the bed.

Carrisa rolls to her side and lifts the covers, inviting him in. "How about you get in here and let me show you just how much I like it."

Vladimir crawls into the bed, dropping the towel onto the floor. He reaches for her, but Carrisa pushes him onto his back and starts to kiss her way down his chest.

"Oh, you like it that much?" Vladimir chuckles.

"Uh, huh." She doesn't say anymore as she positions herself between his legs and takes his growing member into her mouth. She is eager, bringing her lips to the bottom of his shaft and letting it fill her mouth.

Vladimir grips Carrisa's hair with both hands. She starts to work her way around his dick as it grows and hardens, filling her mouth until her lips are stretched out fully. She uses her tongue to work, up and down. With her right palm, she cups his balls and gently squeezes them one at a time while saliva builds up and Vladimir's shaft becomes completely wet.

"Oh, fuck," Vladimir calls out. "Yeah, suck it, just like that, fuck."

They had first slept together on Christmas Eve last year. Vladimir has learned that Carrisa likes for him to take control, and he is all too willing to do so. However, he loved these rare moments where she bends him at her will. Right now, she has complete control, and she knows it.

Carrisa continues to bob her head up and down, letting his dick hit the back of her throat. Every time she comes back up, she makes sure to put extra force behind her sucking; her cheeks caving in with what little room her mouth still has.

When she feels his balls start to tighten, she slowly releases him with a loud POP.

"Is this how it's going to be, like forever?" Vladimir asks breathlessly.

"I imagine that it will get better once I am all old and shit." Carrisa giggles at his perplexed expression. "You know, when my teeth fall out, when I am like eighty or something. It might get better then." She tucks her lips into her teeth and says, "Like this!" They both bust out in hysterics at her display.

Vladimir lets out another boisterous laugh and pulls her up to him. "Get over here."

"I have nowhere else I would rather be," Carrisa says as she positions herself above his throbbing penis.

She slowly works her way onto him, the moisture thick on both of them, ready for entry. She rides her fiancé with a passion she has never felt before. Something new has come alive inside of her. A feeling of love and acceptance that she never had in her life before now. Vladimir can see it in her eyes as she stares down at him. He loves the connection that they have, and he will do everything in his power to make sure it stays there as long as he lives.

They reach climax together, something they often do, but this time it is different. There is a sense of magic in the air around them.

Jalal may have fucked them up for a while, but Vladimir will be eternally grateful for that asshole. If it wasn't for him, Carrisa would have never come to Tyler, and Vladimir would have never found her. He might have been doomed for the rest of his life and forced to live without the feeling that he has right now—the feeling of being complete.

Carrisa drops down onto Vladimir's chest. Panting, she says," I think I might have woken up Topsy."

Vladimir runs a hand over her now damp hair. "Honey, I think you woke my mother, and she is a few miles away."

Carrisa slaps his chest and rolls over to his side. "Oh, please," she lets out a long breath, "Your mom sleeps through anything."

"This is true," Vladimir agrees. "So, my lease is up next month. I was thinking we could move over to a two-bedroom. That way, my critters could have their own room, and you could set up the place the way you want it to be."

"No, that won't work," Carrisa declares.

"No?"

"Nope. I think we need to look for a house. Yep, that is what I want, a house. I want to be your wife and have a real home with you. That way, not only can your "critters"," she says with air quotes, "have their own room, but so can the baby."

Vladimir sits straight up. "Baby?"

"Relax," Carrisa laughs while pulling him back down. "I'm not pregnant, but I do want to have babies right away."

"Babies, as in more than one?" Vladimir questions.

"Yep, lots and lots of babies. Is that okay with you?" Carrisa looks him in the eyes and waits for an answer.

She doesn't have to wait long. Vladimir leans in and gives her a lingering, gentle kiss, then says, "That sounds absolutely divine."

THE END

Acknowledgments

I have a feeling there is still more to come from these Frazier boys. They are interesting characters, and I think each one deserves their own story.

Last year, I took a poll in my fan group, and Vladimir won. I am glad he did because he was very unique and entertaining to work with (because, you know, he is a real person and all).

Thank you to everyone that participated in that poll; I hope you enjoyed his story.

Thank you to my family and friends for always being so supportive and encouraging. You guys give me the greatest material to work with. I want to also thank the writing community and all the wonderful author friends I have made over the past couple of years. You guys are so very special to me, and I am eternally grateful.

To my ARC team. Thank you so very much for sticking with me and constantly giving me valuable feedback while simultaneously stroking my ego.

As always, a massive thank you to my editor and best friend, Mandy Farrar. I would be lost without you so don't ever leave me, okay?

A special thank you to Roxana Coumans with Five Dogs Book Editing for cleaning up and polishing off my mini book baby with your quick proofread!

Connect with the author

Did you enjoy this book? Please leave a review...
https://www.amazon.com/Vladimirs-Victory-Frazier-Family-FRAZIER-ebook/dp/B09PGPZR9B/ref=pd_ybh_a_2?_encoding=UTF8&psc=1&refRID=N4HSCFFZ8EZSX6T2SGNG

Other books by Leigh that you might like...

Girl Bully, a psychological thriller.
https://www.amazon.com/Girl-Bully-Leigh-M-Hall/dp/B08DST1ZG7/ref=pd_ybh_a_4?_encoding=UTF8&psc=1&refRID=BXJKW0HXZCYTSF81YPMW

Girl Vengeance, a Girl Bully novella.
https://www.amazon.com/Girl-Vengeance-Bully-Novella/dp/B08YQCQR1J/ref=pd_ybh_a_3?_encoding=UTF8&psc=1&refRID=1YQ3NRV5DDDVM2D515P9

This Family Sucks! Sincerely Yours, Peter Frazier, a suspense novel.

https://www.amazon.com/Family-Sucks-Sincerely-Yours-Frazier-ebook/dp/B08LVX7LW2/ref=pd_ybh_a_4?_encoding=UTF8&psc=1&refRID=73VZ35S20K40Q581SFHP

Capability, a dramatic psychological thriller.

https://www.amazon.com/dp/B0933L8GBX/ref=nav_timeline_asin?_encoding=UTF8&psc=1

Connect with the author:

https://www.facebook.com/michelle.odell.54379

https://www.instagram.com/leighmhall/

https://www.goodreads.com/user/show/92735739-leigh-hall

author.lmhall@gmail.com

Leigh is a believer in fairytales, the kind that keep some people up at night.

Graduating from the school of hard knocks, she is a realist and always looks for multiple sides to everyone she encounters.

She lives in Texas with her family of gremlins and their amazing dogs. Not only does she love the heat, but she is preparing herself just in case there, in fact, will be a hell at the end of all this.

Because enjoys being alone so much, she spends all her time in the land of fictional characters and keeps her head buried in a book. With ideas continually running around in her strange mind, she decided to dip her toes into writing.

Other books written by Leigh...

Girl Bully

Girl Vengeance

This Family Sucks! Sincerely Yours, Peter Frazier

Vladimir's Victory

Capability

Where The Hell Are We?

Capturing Cadence ~ A Dark Duet Book 1